ABOUT THE ALDEN ALL STARS

Nothing's more important to Derrick, Matt, Josh, and Jesse than their team, the Alden Panthers. Whether the sport is football, hockey, baseball, or track and field, the four seventh-graders can always be found practicing, sweating, and giving their all. Sometimes the Panthers are on their way to a winning season, and sometimes the team can't do anything right. But no matter what, you can be sure the Alden All Stars are playing to win.

"This fast-paced [series] is sure to be a hit with young readers."   —*Publishers Weekly*

"Packed with play-by-play action and snappy dialogue, the text adeptly captures the seventh-grade sports scene."   —*ALA Booklist*

The *Alden All Stars* series:

Duel on the Diamond
Jester in the Backcourt
Shot from Midfield
Last Chance Quarterback
Breaking Loose
Power Play
Setting the Pace
Wild Pitch
Championship Summer

ALDEN ALL STARS

Championship Summer

David Halecroft

PUFFIN BOOKS

PUFFIN BOOKS
Published by the Penguin Group
Viking Penguin, a division of Penguin Books USA Inc.,
375 Hudson Street, New York, New York 10014, U.S.A.
Penguin Books Ltd, 27 Wrights Lane, London W8 5TZ, England
Penguin Books Australia Ltd, Ringwood, Victoria, Australia
Penguin Books Canada Ltd, 2801 John Street, Markham, Ontario, Canada L3R 1B4
Penguin Books (N.Z.) Ltd, 182–190 Wairau Road, Auckland 10, New Zealand

Penguin Books Ltd, Registered Offices: Harmondsworth, Middlesex, England

Published in Puffin Books, 1991
1   3   5   7   9   10   8   6   4   2
Copyright © Daniel Weiss and Associates, 1991
All rights reserved

Library of Congress Catalog Card Number: 91-52573
ISBN 0-14-034808-5

Printed in the United States of America
Set in Century Schoolbook

Championship Summer

1

The trouble started when Matt Greene tried to steal third base.

It was early summer in the town of Cranbrook, and the seventh graders were playing the eighth graders in a pickup baseball game. Matt was on second, with one out. He inched away from the bag, crouching low like a running back. Matt was a speed demon, the fastest sprinter in the conference—and Sam McCaskill, the eighth grade pitcher, knew he wanted to steal.

Sam started from the stretch, checked Matt over his shoulder, and set. Justin Johnson, the eighth grade second baseman, snuck to second behind Matt and got ready for the pickoff throw.

"Matt, watch out!" Jesse Kissler cried from the seventh graders' dugout. "Don't lead off too far! Justin's covering behind you. . . ."

But Matt turned and sprinted for third, just as Sam spun around and hurled the ball to Justin at second. Matt stopped dead in his tracks.

He was caught in a rundown.

Justin ran toward Matt, pumping and faking throws, while the third baseman ran forward. By now, the whole seventh grade bench was standing, shouting advice.

"Hold back," Jesse yelled from the dugout.

"Go for third," Josh Bank called.

Matt turned and sprinted full speed toward third. He was past the third baseman in a split second, with nothing but wide-open dirt between him and a stolen base. It looked like he was about to get himself out of the rundown.

Justin brought his arm back and whipped the ball.

The throw hit Matt squarely in the back and he dropped to the dirt. The third baseman picked up the ball and tagged him out.

"You hit him on purpose!" Josh Bank screamed, running out onto the field. "You threw that ball right into his back!"

Josh Bank was thin and wiry, with bright red hair. He had a great sense of humor, but it didn't take much to get him mad. "You guys are playing dirty ball!" he yelled, right into Justin's face.

"We are not," Justin answered, as Matt got up slowly from the ground.

"You're a liar," Josh yelled, stepping closer. "You hit Matt on purpose, because he was going to steal third. You guys are sore losers, that's what you are!" he said, giving Justin a little push in the chest.

"You better lay off, Josh," Justin said, as eighth graders started gathering around them, "or you'll be sorry."

Jesse Kissler, the seventh grade pitcher, could tell that things were about to get out of hand. He jogged over from the bench and, without saying a word, dragged Josh back toward the dugout.

"We can't let them get away with that," Josh said, as Jesse pulled him away. "They're playing dirty ball."

Jesse knew all about Josh's temper. They had been on the football team together that fall. Jesse had been the quarterback, and Josh had been the wide receiver. He knew that Josh would cool off in a few minutes, and everything would be fine again.

"I've got an idea," Josh said to Jesse, as they sat down on the bench. "Start shaving the eighth graders with your pitches. You know, pitch them really close. . . ."

"No way, Josh," Jesse said, shaking his head. "Things are bad enough. If I start shaving batters, we're going to have an all-out brawl."

"But you saw what they did to Matt!" Josh said.

"The best revenge," Jesse said, "is beating the eighth graders fair and square."

A minute later, Jesse jogged out to the mound and retired the eighth graders, one, two, three. His pitching arm felt great today, and it helped having one of his best friends, Derrick Larson, catching behind the plate. Derrick had moved to Cranbrook from Minnesota at the beginning of the school year. He had blond hair that was almost white, bright blue eyes, and a strong Minnesota accent. He had been the star of the Alden hockey team, and he was a great catcher and hitter.

Jesse led off the inning for the seventh graders. He grabbed his favorite bat—a Louisville Slugger, Bo Jackson model—dropped his donut weight around it, and took a few practice swings. Sam and Dennis Clements, the eighth grade catcher, were standing on the mound having a conference. When they were done, Jesse knocked the weight from his bat and strolled out to the batter's box. He glanced up at Sam on the mound, and saw that Sam was wearing a funny little smile.

I wonder what he's planning, Jesse thought as he cocked his bat.

It didn't take long to find out. Sam's first pitch was way inside, and Jesse had to drop to the dirt to get out of the way.

"Keep the ball over the plate, McCaskill," Josh shouted angrily from the on-deck circle.

Jesse tried to keep his cool. He was a pitcher, and he could tell when he was being shaved too close. He cocked his bat again, and stared right into Sam's eyes.

Sam wound up and pitched. The ball flew inside again, and Jesse had to twist to avoid getting hit. He looked back at the seventh grade bench, and could see that everyone was standing up, yelling out at Sam to put the ball over the plate.

The third pitch looked like a strike, and Jesse started his cut. At the last minute, though, the pitch curved sharply inside and jammed Jesse's swing. He hit the ball on the handle of the bat, and the ball looped weakly over the infield. Jesse took off running.

It looked like the ball might drop into shallow

center field for a single, but Nick Wilkerson, the eighth grade center fielder, was running full speed toward the ball. Jesse wasn't the fastest guy on earth, and he knew he'd have to hustle to make first. The ball hit the grass right at Nick's feet, and Nick picked it up on the short hop. Still running at full speed, Nick pulled the ball from his glove, jumped up high in the air, then twisted and chucked the ball to first.

The first baseman had one toe on the bag, and the rest of his body stretched out for the throw. Jesse heard the ball smack into the first baseman's glove a split second before his foot touched the bag. He was out.

Nick had made an incredible play. Nabbing a short hop at full speed was one of the hardest things to do in all of baseball. Since Nick was one of Jesse's friends, Jesse tipped his hat to him as he jogged back toward the bench. Nick smiled and nodded in return.

Josh stopped Jesse at the on-deck circle.

"If Sam pitches me inside," Josh said, adjusting his batting helmet over his cycling cap, "there's going to be trouble. These guys think they own the world."

"Keep your cool," Jesse said, patting Josh on the shoulder. "Remember, the best revenge is winning."

Josh stepped up to the plate and cocked his bat. Sam wound up and pitched so far inside that Josh had to hit the dirt. When he got up, his face was red with anger.

The next pitch curved inside again. Josh ducked to avoid it, but he wasn't fast enough, and the ball smacked him on the shoulder and bounced to the ground.

Instead of jogging to first base, Josh picked up the ball and chucked it as hard as he could at Sam. Sam was so surprised that he didn't have time to react, and the ball smacked him in the thigh.

It didn't take much to get Sam angry, either, and he took off running toward Josh. By now, both teams were standing up in the dugouts, waiting to pour onto the field for a fight. Josh met Sam with a punch to the shoulder, and then the two boys threw a flurry of hooks and uppercuts. Dennis, the eighth grade catcher, stepped in and broke it up, just as the others raced off the benches.

The two teams lined up and faced each other across home plate, clenching their fists and shouting.

"We should have known it was a dumb idea to play *real* baseball with a bunch of babies," Sam said.

"At least we play fair," Derrick jeered.

"Just because you're losing . . ." Justin responded, taking a step forward and pushing Josh.

"You guys think you own the world," Josh called, pushing Justin right back.

"Okay, okay," Jesse said, walking out between the two sides. "Let's break it up."

"That's right," Nick said, stepping out from the eighth grade line. "Let's just forget this game."

Jesse turned around, gathered all his teammates, and led them off the field. Nick did the same with the eighth graders.

Jesse couldn't believe how close they had just come to an all-out, punch-throwing, cleat-kicking brawl. One thing was for sure, that was the last time they'd ever play the eighth graders.

2

The next day, Jesse was cutting the grass when his mother opened the front door and waved. It was a hot summer day, and Jesse was happy to take a break.

"Telephone, Jesse," Mrs. Kissler called, cupping her hands around her mouth. His mother usually didn't call him when he was working in the yard, so Jesse knew the call must be important.

He turned off the mower and jogged toward the house. Jesse was tall, with a sandy blond crew cut and arms and legs that seemed a little too long. Even though he had a funny, clumsy way of running, Jesse was a good athlete. He had been the starting pitcher on the seventh grade baseball team that spring and—after a rough start—had helped lead the team to a conference championship.

Jesse hurried to the phone in the kitchen, and picked up the receiver.

"Hello?"

"Did you get the letter in the mail?" Josh asked right away.

"What letter?" Jesse asked.

"The letter about the Junior High Baseball Invitational," Josh answered. He sounded very excited, and started talking a mile a minute. "There's a new statewide tournament, and if we win our division, we get to go to Simpson City and play in Simpson City Stadium. Coach Lanigan is going to be our coach, and if we win the whole tournament we get a huge trophy that's . . ."

"Whoa, you're talking too fast," Jesse said with a laugh. He looked down at the kitchen table, and sitting right at his place was a letter from the athletic department of Alden Junior High with his name on it. He snatched it and opened it up.

"Wouldn't it be the greatest thing to travel all the

way to Simpson City, and play baseball in a *real* big-league stadium?" Josh asked.

"But you weren't even on the baseball team this spring," Jesse said, as he read the form letter. "You were on the track team."

"Read the rules," Josh said. "The tryouts are open to anyone, whether they played on the baseball team or not. I guess every guy in school got the same letter."

As Jesse read on, he couldn't believe his eyes. Everything that Josh said was true. Coach Lanigan was holding tryouts starting in two days. The team that he selected would then play in a state divisional tournament. The winner of the divisionals would get to go to Simpson City, the capital of the state, for the finals. Jesse couldn't believe how great it sounded.

Then he read the print at the bottom of the page.

"Uh-oh," Jesse said, the smile suddenly vanishing from his face.

"What's wrong?" Josh asked.

"It says here that the tryouts are for seventh and eighth graders," Jesse answered.

"What? You mean we'll be on the same team?" Josh cried.

"We better meet at Pete's Pizza this afternoon," Jesse said. "We need a plan."

"I'll call Matt and Derrick," Josh said. "We'll all meet at Pete's at three o'clock."

Jesse hung up the phone and sat for a while. He read the letter over and over again. There was no doubt that the tournament sounded amazing.

But how in the world were they going to get along with the eighth graders?

About a half-hour later, Jesse was standing in the kitchen, gulping down a glass of orange juice, when he heard a knock at the front door.

Nick Wilkerson was Jesse's next door neighbor. He stood in the doorway holding his copy of Coach's letter in one hand, and a stack of baseball cards in the other.

"What's up?" Jesse said with a smile, as Nick stepped inside.

Jesse and Nick were old friends. Jesse had always looked up to Nick, because Nick was a year older and seemed to know everything about everything. Nick knew how to use a drill and an electric saw, and he knew how engines worked. The only thing Jesse knew more about than Nick was baseball cards. Jesse had one of the best collections at Alden Junior High, with over 600 cards. Nick only had 100 cards in his collection.

Nick came over a couple of times a week, just to sit around and trade cards. Nick wasn't big, but he was really quick and was a great all-around athlete. He had dirty-blond hair, wore glasses, and was famous for his jokes. As far as Jesse was concerned, it didn't matter that Nick was an eighth grader—he liked him anyway.

"Did you get the letter about the tournament?" Nick asked.

"Yeah," Jesse answered. "The tournament sounds pretty awesome."

The two friends sat on the family room floor, as Jesse pulled out a shoe box filled with baseball cards. They were all neatly wrapped into bunches, one bunch for each major league team.

"It sure does," Nick said as he laid his own cards on the floor. "But we're probably the only players on the two sides who don't hate each other."

"I know," Jesse said, leaning down to study Nick's cards. "Maybe we can do something about it."

"Well, we have to win the divisionals, so we can take that trip to Simpson City," Nick said, flipping through one of Jesse's huge stack of cards. "And to do that, we need a truce between the two teams. Otherwise, we'll never win the state trophy." Nick glanced up from the baseball cards and looked Jesse right in the eyes. "We're the only two people who can bring the teams together."

"I'm meeting my friends at Pete's this afternoon," Jesse said. "I'll talk to them then."

When Jesse got to Pete's that afternoon, Josh, Matt, and Derrick were wolfing down a large pizza with everything on it. As soon as Jesse sat down, Josh opened his mouth to talk.

"I know what you're going to say," Jesse began, before Josh could even say a word. "You're going to say that we can't play on the same team with the eighth graders."

"We *can't*," Josh said.

"But we have to," Jesse answered, grabbing a slice of pizza. "If we want to make it to the state championship, we have to play together as a team."

"You're crazy," Josh responded. "Sam hit me with a pitch on purpose."

"And Justin hit me in the back with a throw," Matt added.

"I know," Jesse said, trying to calm down his friends. "Those guys play a little rough. But we don't really have a choice."

"Yes, we do," Josh said, leaning closer. "We can tell all of the seventh graders to play especially hard in the tryouts, and make sure none of the eighth graders make the team."

"Dream on, Josh," Jesse answered with a laugh. "The eighth graders won their division this year. They've got a lot of great players, and Coach can't cut them all."

"Or we could poke holes in all of their bike tires so they can't make it to practice. . . ." Josh suggested.

"Give it up," Jesse said.

By the time they left Pete's and headed for the Game Place, all the boys were ready to give the eighth graders a second chance.

"We need a truce," Jesse said.

"But only because we want to win in Simpson City," Josh added.

"Wait a second," Derrick said, smiling. "We better make the team first, or we'll never even *see* Simpson City!"

3

"Remember to cheer for the eighth graders," Jesse told his friends, before they hit the field for the first day of tryouts. "If we have to play together, we might as well start acting like a team now."

"It's not going to be easy," Josh said, tying his cleats. "I still think they're a bunch of buttheads."

Jesse gave Josh a look. Josh smiled and shrugged.

Jesse knew it wasn't going to be easy for the two grades to get along. He hoped that Nick had talked to his friends, too, and that the eighth graders wouldn't come to the tryouts thinking that they owned the world.

Jesse saw Nick walking toward the diamond, carrying his bat and glove. Justin, Sam, and Dennis were walking with him, toting a big green bag of bats and a stack of white bases. Jesse jogged up to the group of eighth graders, his heart thumping nervously in his chest.

"Hey," Jesse said, falling in beside Nick. "Are you guys psyched to go to Simpson City?"

At first, Justin, Sam, and Dennis gave Jesse the cold shoulder. They didn't look at him, and they didn't say a word. Then Nick elbowed Justin in the ribs, and Justin rolled his eyes.

"Yeah, we're going to clean up in Simpson City," Justin said halfheartedly.

"Yeah," Sam added, in a quiet voice. "Simpson City is ours."

Jesse could tell that the eighth graders were still mad, but at least they were trying to keep the peace. He gave Nick a little wink, and Nick smiled back and gave a thumbs-up.

"Listen up, everyone," Coach Lanigan called out a minute later, rapping his knuckles on his clipboard. All the boys gathered around Coach at home plate, the eighth graders on one side and the seventh graders on the other

"I'm glad to see so many of you trying out for the invitational team," Coach began. Coach Lanigan was a big man, with black hair and a deep voice. "I'm also glad to see some boys who didn't play baseball trying out, like Josh Bank and Matt Greene, our local track stars."

"Hey, I was part of the field events," Ed Bannister called out. "I was shot-put king." He puffed out his chest and pretended to hurl a shot put in the air. "That's a record-breaking distance."

Bruce Judge and Andrew Isaacs, who had both been on the track team, lifted Bannister as if he were a champion. But the two of them quickly collapsed under Bannister's heavy weight.

Coach laughed. "You all have real spirit and I like that. Unfortunately, there are going to have to be some cuts. Not all of you can play on the team, so I need to see what you can do. Today, we're going to work on fielding and baserunning. Let me see your best effort."

"Excuse me, Coach Lanigan," said a boy whom no one had ever seen before. He had black eyes and dark brown hair, and wore jeans and a T-shirt.

"My name is B. J. Carruthers," the boy continued. "I just moved here from North Colby."

At the words "North Colby," a hiss went up from all the boys, both seventh and eighth graders alike. North Colby was Alden's fiercest competitor, and playing with a kid from North Colby was like playing with an enemy spy. When B. J. heard the hissing, his face turned red.

"North Colby is a thousand times better than Alden," B. J. said angrily, looking around at all the boys. "Alden stinks."

"Then why are you trying out for our team?" Sam said, from the eighth grade side.

"Yeah, why don't you just go back home?" Josh said.

"I would if I could," B. J. answered. "But if I want to go to Simpson City, I guess I'll have to play on this stupid team. And I *do* plan to go to Simpson City."

"Okay, okay," Coach Lanigan said, before anyone could say another word. "Welcome to Cranbrook, B. J. Why don't you jog out to the infield, and we'll see what you can do. Everyone else, take a place in the infield or the outfield. We'll be rotating, so it doesn't matter where you start."

The players spread out on the field. Coach Lanigan stood at home plate, tossed a ball up, and smacked a sharp grounder right to the new kid. B. J. backed up from it and put his glove down, keeping his chin way up in the air.

The ball went right between his legs.

"Nice play, North Colby," Matt called out sarcastically.

"Yeah, nice play," Justin echoed.

"Why don't you shut up?" B. J. said to them. "Just wait, and you'll see what I can do."

Jesse could tell it would be a pain to have this new kid around. B. J. seemed to think he was better than everyone else on the field, just because he was from North Colby. On the other hand, the seventh and eighth graders at least agreed on their dislike of B. J. If they could agree on that, maybe they could start getting along in other ways, too.

Coach smacked another grounder to Eddie Peres, a seventh grader who was playing shortstop. Eddie hustled toward the ball, backhanded it, then leaped into the air and whipped the ball to first. The throw was low, and bounced in the dirt—but Derrick stretched out from first base, kept his foot on the bag, and snatched the ball on the short hop. It was a great play, and two seventh graders had done it.

"Good pickup, Derrick," Sam said from the eighth grade side.

"Yeah, nice backhand, Eddie," Justin called out.

Jesse smiled. Maybe the truce really was working.

"That was heads-up ball," Coach said, as the players rotated their positions. "On this play, I want you to pretend there are runners on first and second. Go for the force-outs."

Coach smacked a hard, bouncing grounder, right down the third-base line. Justin dove for it, back-handed the ball in midair, and landed in the dirt a few feet from the base. He scrambled to his feet, touched the bag to force the runner out, then twisted and chucked the ball toward second.

Matt was covering second, waiting on the base with his glove up. But Justin's throw was high, and Matt had to jump for it. No one thought Matt had a chance to make the catch—but they had forgotten that Matt was a sprinter, with the most powerful legs in the conference. He jumped straight up, three feet in the air, and stretched his arm up as high as he could. The ball smacked into the web of his glove, and Matt dropped onto the base for the imaginary out at second.

Matt twisted and pumped the throw to first. B. J. Carruthers was covering first, standing up straight with one foot right in the middle of the bag. Matt's throw was picture perfect, and if B. J. caught it, the team would complete an amazing triple play.

B. J., seeing the ball speeding toward his face, kept his glove up, but turned his face away. The ball zomed right over his shoulder and rolled into foul territory.

"The sun was in my eyes," B. J. said.

"Yeah, right," Nick answered, looking up into the sky. "I guess that means you have eyes in the back of your head."

Everyone broke up laughing, seventh and eighth graders alike. B. J. gave Nick a laser-beam stare, and Nick stared right back.

"Good cooperation, Justin and Matt," Coach called out. "B. J., the ball's not going to hurt you if you keep your eye on it. But it might hurt you if you look away."

Next, Coach smacked a soaring, incredibly high fly ball into right-center field, and Jesse ran toward it. Out of the corner of his eye he could see Nick running toward it, too. Jesse was a pitcher, and he really didn't like to field. He would have been happy to let Nick grab this one.

"Take it, Jesse," Nick said, stopping in his tracks. "This one's yours."

Jesse felt his heart come into his throat. The ball was a black dot way up in the blue sky, as he ran to the place where he thought it would land. Then he realized he had run too far forward, and turned around and ran back. The ball kept falling, faster and faster, and Jesse ran forward again, feeling a cold sweat break out on his forehead.

Now the ball looked like it would drop *behind* him,

so Jesse ran backward again, stumbling over his feet and falling onto the grass. The ball smacked into the ground five feet away. He picked it up, burning with embarrassment, and hurled the ball all the way to Dennis at the plate.

"At least it was a perfect throw," Nick said.

"I'm a pitcher," Jesse answered. "Not an out-fielder."

After forty-five minutes of fielding practice, Coach decided it was time for some baserunning drills.

"I want you to do some wind sprints," Coach began, as the boys lined up along the right field foul line.

Everyone looked over to Matt and Josh, who were both wearing little grins. Matt had won the confer-ence championship in the 100 meter dash that spring, and Josh had been a big help in the 4 × 100 meter relay team. Even if they weren't the greatest fielders ever, this would give them their chance to shine for Coach Lanigan.

"It's not fair," Jesse teased, squatting down beside Matt. "You guys are track stars."

"On your mark, get set . . . go!" Coach shouted.

Jesse sprang forward, pumped his arms, and tried to make his legs go as fast as they could—but Matt and Josh shot ahead of him like bullets. They were already across the finish line by the time Jesse had huffed and puffed to the 75-yard line. In fact, Jesse was almost the last player to finish.

The only one to finish after him was B. J. Carruthers, and B. J. looked mad.

"I hate this place," B. J. muttered, under his breath.

"What did you say?" Josh said, walking up to B. J. and looking him right in the eye.

A couple of eighth graders also walked over and stared at B. J. He stared right back, laughed, then turned away.

4

"That kid B. J.'s got a chip on his shoulder," Matt said the next day, as he spread his baseball cards out on the grass. "He should move back to North Colby."

"I can't wait to see the scene he'll make when he gets cut," Derrick added with a smile. "B. J.'s the only guy I've ever met who has a worse temper than Josh."

"Hey, what did you say?" Josh said, bringing his fist back as if he was going to smack Derrick. Then he gave him a friendly pat on the shoulder and started laughing.

Jesse, Derrick, Josh, and Matt were in Jesse's backyard, playing for baseball cards. All four friends had big collections, with lots of old cards from their fathers' collections, too.

Matt jogged over to the fence and set an empty soda can on top of the post. Everybody put one of their baseball cards in a pile, and then picked up pebbles and stones from the gravel along the edges of Jesse's backyard. The first one to knock the can off the fence would win all four baseball cards.

"It's funny, but the two grades have been getting along great since B. J. showed up," Jesse said, hurling a stone at the can, and missing. "I guess he's somebody we can *all* get mad at."

"It's pretty hard to move to a new place, though," Derrick said, taking aim with his stone. "I feel sort of sorry for him." Derrick hurled the stone, and the four friends watched it slice through the air. He knew what it was like to move to a place where there are already lots of cliques and large groups of friends.

His stone made a big curve and hit the middle of the can with a *ping!* The can jumped from the fence and fell to the ground.

"Yes!" Derrick cried, reaching down to snatch up

the stack of cards. "You know what, I say we give B. J. a break," Derrick said, flipping through his new cards. "If he wants to be a jerk, that's up to him."

"I agree," Jesse said. "It's his choice."

Jesse jogged to the fence, picked up the can, and put it back on the fence post. Jesse was almost glad that B. J. Carruthers was trying out for the team. Without B. J., Jesse figured that the feud between the two grades would come right back to life.

It was almost a hundred degrees during the second tryout later that afternoon.

"We're going to work on pitching and hitting today," Coach Lanigan called out. "Everyone who's interested in pitching or catching, come over to the bullpen. The rest of you, spread out on the field and shag hits."

Jesse hurried over to the bullpen—wearing a Cubs cap that Nick had once given him, for good luck—and Derrick walked beside him carrying his catcher's equipment. Jesse and Derrick had been a good pitcher-catcher combination last spring, and Jesse was hoping to get a position as a starter. So was Sam McCaskill, the best pitcher in the eighth grade. Sam was a natural leader—as well as a fast, controlled pitcher—and Jesse was worried that he might dominate the mound.

"Are you ready to see some pitching?" Sam said to Jesse, as they walked up to the rubber. "And I mean *real* pitching, not that wimpy stuff you seventh graders throw."

Jesse felt his face go red. He didn't want to get into an argument with Sam—but it was awfully hard to let a comment like that pass. Just as he was about to come back with a sharp reply, B. J. Carruthers ran up to the mound.

"Are *you* trying out for pitcher?" Sam asked B. J.

"Sure," B. J. said, with a sneer. "I'll bet I can outthrow anyone in Cranbrook."

Sam threw his head back and laughed. "We'll see about that, bigshot."

"Okay, men," Coach began, as he walked toward the mound with a bag of balls. "I know most of you have pitched before, so I'll just remind you that baseball is seventy-five percent pitching, which means the pitcher is the most important person on the field. And a good pitcher needs a good catcher."

Jesse watched Sam's motion as Sam pitched. Sam was smooth, with a slow, high kick and a fast delivery. He had a good curve and a pretty good changeup, but his fastball was his best pitch. Jesse was worried that it might even be as fast as *his* fastball.

When it was Jesse's turn, Derrick put on his catcher's mask and squatted down behind the plate. It had been over three weeks since the end of the season, and it took a few pitches for Jesse's arm to loosen up. He threw a couple of his curves into the dirt, but made up for that by chucking his fastballs so fast that Derrick had to take off his mitt and shake the sting out of his hand.

"Okay, B. J.," Coach said, after Jesse had finished his round. "Show us what you can do."

B. J. took to the mound. Derrick crouched behind the plate and raised his mitt for a target. B. J. stepped back, turned on the rubber, and lifted his arms above his head. He delivered the pitch with a yell, but the ball went ten feet over Derrick's head and hit the backstop.

Jesse and Sam both lifted their gloves up to hide their laughter from Coach.

"You're trying to throw too hard, B. J.," Coach said.

"I know what I'm doing," B. J. answered under his breath.

B. J.'s next pitch wasn't any better, and his face turned redder and redder. He really *was* the only person Jesse had ever met with a temper worse than Josh's. When B. J. tossed another one into the back-stop, he chucked his glove to the dirt.

"That's enough, B. J.," Coach said sternly. "Move over for the next pitcher."

Duane Potter, an eighth grader, was the next pitcher, but he wasn't as good as Sam. After Duane had pitched his round, Coach said it was time for batting practice. Coach told Sam to take the mound, and set up a batting rotation so that everyone would get a chance at the plate.

Jesse was the first to bat. The last time he had faced Sam, Sam had started shaving his pitches too close. Jesse knew that Sam wouldn't do that in front of Coach, and all he cared about now was whacking the ball out of the field.

Jesse cocked his bat and gazed up the alley at Sam. Sam wound up, delivered, and Jesse saw the fastball speed toward the strike zone. He swung, felt the ball hit the sweet spot, and watched it go sailing out of the infield. It was a deep, solid hit to right.

Justin was playing right field, and he turned around and ran backward, looking over his shoulder like a wide receiver. Jesse sprinted to first, then used the bag to send himself off toward second. Justin faded back, keeping his eye on the high pop fly. At the last moment he dove, reached his glove out as far as he could, and snagged the ball in the webbing just before it hit the ground.

Jesse looked out into right field and tipped his cap to Justin. It was a great catch.

Next, B. J. stepped up to the plate and everyone started cheering for Sam on the mound—both seventh and eighth graders.

B. J. stood stiffly in the box, holding the bat straight up in the air. He swung and missed the first pitch by a mile.

"Bend your knees, B. J.," Coach called out, "loosen up."

B. J. didn't budge. The second pitch was too high, but B. J. took a wild swing for strike two—and the whole field started whistling and cheering. B. J. looked angry as he got settled for the third pitch. The pitch was way low, but B. J. went fishing for it, pulling his head up and missing the ball for strike three.

B. J. hammered his bat against home plate, then tossed it into the fence by the dugout.

"You're not impressing anyone with your temper, B. J.," Coach said. "Try to keep your cool. Also, try to keep your head down and your eyes on the ball when you swing. If you pull your head up, you'll never make contact."

"He should go back to North Colby," Jesse said.

"With a temper like that," Matt answered, "there's no telling what the guy will do."

A few minutes later, Jesse strolled to the mound and faced his first batter, Nick Wilkerson. Jesse wound up and delivered a fastball, right at Derrick's mitt. Nick took an easy swing, and a solid *crack!* rang out in the air.

Jesse's heart dropped as he watched the ball sail out over Josh's head in left field. Josh turned on the speed, but couldn't get to the ball before it hit the grass. He chucked the ball to the cutoff man, and the cutoff man hurled it to Derrick at home—but Nick had already slid across the plate for a home run.

After everyone had batted twice, Coach called the team over to the plate.

"I've been watching everyone very carefully these past two days," Coach began, looking at his clipboard. "All of you have good ability. Unfortunately, not all of you can be on the team. Cutting players is always the hardest thing for a coach to do, but four of you boys won't be playing on the team. Ed Bannister, Bruce Judge, Andrew Isaacs, and B. J. Carruthers."

"What?" B. J. shouted, throwing his glove down. "Are you kidding? This lousy team doesn't deserve to go to Simpson City, anyway. I've had enough of Cranbrook, and everyone in it. This whole place stinks."

"Hey . . ." Josh and Sam said together, stepping toward B. J.

"Alden doesn't have a chance of winning the divisionals," B. J. said.

At that, B. J. picked up his glove, ran off the field, and disappeared into the woods. Coach Lanigan watched him go, shaking his head.

"He'll get over it," Coach said, looking at his clipboard. "I haven't decided which positions you'll be playing yet, but here's the final roster for the invitational team: Dennis Clements, Josh Bank, Duane Potter, Eddie Peres, Sam McCaskill, Jesse Kissler, Nick Wilkerson, Derrick Larson, Justin Johnson, Matt Greene, Kyle Bushmiller, David Hilary, Drew Smith, Benny Chapman, and Sy Steinbergen. We have a darn good team, but we have to get ready to win our first divisional game next Wednesday, against Williamsport. That's only a week away. What do you say, men? Are we going to win?"

"Yes!" everyone shouted.

"Good," Coach said. "Let's hear it for the new Panthers!"

5

Nick swung hard at Jesse's fastball, and laced a hot line drive down the third-base line. Justin, playing third, dove to his side but the ball was just beyond his glove. He landed on his stomach in a cloud of dust, and the ball sailed into open territory.

Sam, who had been at second after a stand-up double, was rounding third and heading for home.

It was the first practice of the new Alden Panthers Invitational team—and Jesse wasn't having a good day on the mound. He sprinted home and stood behind Derrick, to back up the play at home plate.

Dennis bare-handed the ball in left field and whipped it toward home. The throw came in low and bounced in the dirt just as Sam dropped for a hook slide into the plate. Sam cut Derrick's legs out from under him and Derrick tumbled into the dust. The ball skipped past him and Jesse backhanded it in the webbing of his glove.

"Nick's going for three!" Coach called out.

Jesse snatched the ball from his glove and hurled the ball to Justin at third base. The throw was perfect, and it should have been an easy out. But Justin didn't drop his glove quickly enough, and Nick slid in safely for a triple.

Jesse walked angrily back to the mound. He was angry at himself for giving up a hit, and he was angry at Justin. He was sure that Justin had delayed the tag on purpose, so that he wouldn't have to tag Nick out. It looked like a sure case of the eighth graders battling the seventh graders—even though they were on the same team.

Jesse finished off the inning, and then Coach Lanigan called the whole team over for a conference. Coach told everyone to have a seat in the grass, and then he knelt down on one knee.

"I think we have a great team here, men," Coach said, looking around. The eighth graders were sitting apart from the seventh graders. They looked like two different teams. "Both the seventh and the eighth grade teams won championships this spring. So the two teams together should clean up in the divisional tournament. No team in the conference will be able to lay a hand on us. Right?"

Everyone cheered.

"Things will be a lot different once we get to Simpson City for the finals," Coach went on. "The competition there is going to be fierce, and we're going to have to play hard if we want to win."

"Coach?" Josh asked, raising his hand. "How big is the trophy that we're going to win in Simpson City?"

Coach laughed. "I like your spirit, Josh. But we've got four games to play before we even get to Simpson City, so let's concentrate on winning those. And one other thing," Coach added, standing up. "If—I mean *when*—we win the divisional title, you boys are going to have to earn some money for the trip to Simpson City. Two hundred dollars, to be exact."

"Two hundred dollars?" everyone said, their mouths dropping open.

"That's right," Coach said. "That money will help cover the cost of traveling to Simpson City. If you don't earn the money, you won't be able to go."

"We could have a car wash," Matt suggested.

"Or we could set up batting cages," Sam said.

"My dad has an old Model-T Ford, and he could give rides in it," Josh added.

"Okay, okay," Coach said, raising his hand with a smile. "We have to win the divisionals first. That means we have to beat Williamsport next Wednesday. Let's get to work!"

After drilling the Panthers in fielding and hitting, Coach divided up the team into two scrimmage sides. Each side was made up of half eighth graders and half seventh graders. Sam was pitching for one side, and Jesse was pitching for the other.

"I want to see you play hard," Coach said, as he tossed a new ball out to Sam on the mound. "Play like you're in Simpson City."

Justin led off and dribbled a grounder back to Sam, who tossed the ball to Matt at first, for an easy out. The second out came when David Hilary popped up to left. Jesse was third in the lineup, and he walked to the plate eager to take a swipe at Sam's pitching.

Jesse cocked his bat and gazed up the alley at Sam. The first pitch came in around the knees. Jesse liked them low. He took a big cut, keeping his eye right on the ball, and connected with a sharp grounder to first. Matt ran to his right and backhanded the ball on the short hop, deep in the infield. He was too far away from the base to make the tag himself, so Sam rushed over from the mound, holding out his glove as he ran.

Jesse and Sam were each running right toward first base, at top speed. Matt hurled the ball, and Sam caught it just as the two boys slammed into each other. The ball flew out of Sam's glove, and Sam went sprawling onto the ground. Jesse's legs were cut out from under him, and he flew forward, landing on his stomach in foul territory.

Both boys were fine, and Jesse was safe with a single. The collision was an accident, but still, Sam gave Jesse a cold stare as he walked back toward the mound.

What's his problem? Jesse thought, as he took his lead off the base.

Josh stepped up to the plate next, with two down and Jesse on first. Josh had a surprising amount of power for his size, but the eighth graders in the outfield didn't know that. They saw Josh's thin, wiry body, and moved in toward the infield.

Josh connected on the third pitch, sending a high fly ball over Nick's head in center field. As soon as Jesse knew for sure that Nick wouldn't catch it, he took off running for second, keeping an eye on the play. Just as Jesse rounded second and headed for third, Josh was rounding first and heading for a close play at second base.

Nick scooped up the ball, turned around, and hurled it as hard and fast as he could. Josh was only a few steps away from second when he saw that the throw was heading right for his knees. He jumped up in the air, and the ball just barely missed his cleats. He landed on top of Eddie Peres, a seventh grader who was covering second base, and the two friends hit the infield in a tangle.

Jesse saw that the ball was loose, rolling toward the empty mound. He decided to take a chance and head for home, keeping his eyes fixed on Dennis, the eighth grade catcher, who was blocking the baseline. Dennis stood there with his mask off, crouching down like a linebacker on a football field. Jesse wondered how he was going to get through Dennis to the plate.

Jesse dropped down for the slide but Dennis crouched down and slammed into him, knocking Jesse's head back. Jesse felt his head hit the hard dirt, and then he felt Dennis's catcher's mitt slap down against his stomach.

"Out!" Coach called. "But watch out, Dennis. You were blocking the baseline, and in a real game you'd be called for interference."

Jesse got up slowly, his head still ringing. Dennis had really given him a good hard whack. As he walked away from the plate, he muttered, "You're a jerk, Dennis."

Dennis gave him a little smile that made Jesse want to slug him in the nose. Jesse knew that he was supposed to help keep the truce between the grades. But it was different when an eighth grader played rough with *him*.

He saw Josh running off the field from second base, and could tell that Josh was mad, too.

"Nick tried to hit me with the throw from center field," Josh said, as they grabbed their gloves from the bench. "If I hadn't jumped, that ball would have smacked me in the knee. I swear I'm going to . . ."

"The eighth graders have gone too far this time," Jesse said, as he rubbed his sore head. "Dennis blocked the plate and slammed into me intentionally."

"Who do those jerks think they are?" Josh said.

"What did you call us?" Justin asked. He was standing next to Josh, getting a drink from the water cooler.

"I said all of you eighth graders are jerks," Josh answered, turning right around and looking Justin in the eye.

"You're asking for it, Bank," Justin answered.

"Yeah, right," Jesse said, still rubbing his head. "We give you guys a chance, and all you do is throw balls at us and block us on the base path."

Before Justin could make another comment, Jesse headed off to the mound. He couldn't believe what jerks the eighth graders were being. Even Nick had tried to throw a ball at Josh.

No more Mr. Nice Guy, Jesse thought as he picked up the rosin bag on the mound.

The first batter Jesse met was Nick. Jesse wanted to give Nick a little scare, and throw some balls way inside. But he knew that Coach would pick up on it, so he pitched his best fastball instead. Nick got hold of his second pitch for a deep fly ball into right field.

Nick rounded first as Josh ran out from the infield to the shallow outfield, to get the cutoff throw. When Nick rounded second and sprinted toward third, Josh was still waving for the ball at the cutoff position. Josh finally snagged the throw, turned, and chucked the ball right at Nick. The throw smacked Nick in the rear end, and sent him sprawling safely onto third base.

Nick stood up, turned around, and stared at Josh.

Josh stared back at Nick, and Jesse could tell that the truce had just been officially broken.

The seventh grade and the eighth grade were now at war.

6

Three days later, on the evening before the first divisional game, Jesse, Josh, Matt, and Derrick were walking home from the Game Place. It was already nine o'clock, but the summer sky was still light, and fireflies were flashing in the shadows of the big trees. Off in the distance, Jesse could hear the chimes of an ice-cream truck as it wound through the streets of Cranbrook. Usually, the friends would have run off to find the truck, and buy ice cream sandwiches and rocket pops. Tonight, they had something else on their minds.

"Williamsport will be a pushover tomorrow," Matt said, as they strolled along. "I don't know what you're worried about."

"Yeah, Jesse," Derrick added. "Williamsport doesn't have a chance against your pitching. They've always had a lousy team."

"I know," Jesse answered, halfheartedly. "I'm psyched to be starting tomorrow, but I just wish you could catch for me." He nudged Derrick in the side. "Dennis will probably try to screw me up."

"I wish I could catch, too," Derrick said, shrugging. "But what Coach says, goes."

"Yeah, we're not just trying to beat Williamsport," Matt said. "We have to beat the eighth graders, too. We have to show them who's in charge of the Alden Panthers."

"Yeah, get psyched, Jesse," Josh said, slapping Jesse on the back. "We're going to carry the Panthers all the way to Simpson City!"

Jesse hoped his friends were right. The last three days of practice had been weird. If anything, the two grades were more angry with each other than ever before. Jesse had been thinking so much about the feud with the eighth graders, that he hadn't been pitching well at practice.

Still, Williamsport was one of the worst teams in

the division and Jesse didn't think he'd have any problem beating them.

The game was held early the next afternoon on the Alden Junior High field. Jesse showed up early and saw that B. J. Carruthers was sitting alone in the bleachers. Jesse figured that B. J. would show up at all the games, just to cheer for the other side. B. J. gave Jesse a cold stare, but Jesse ignored him. There were more important things to worry about than B. J.

Coach Lanigan was taking bases and bats out of the new storage shed by the diamond.

"Hey, Coach," Jesse said, grabbing a bag of bats. "Could Derrick catch for me? I pitched with him all last season."

"The roster is set," Coach said. "Besides, you need to be able to work with different catchers."

"But . . ."

"No buts," Coach answered, closing the door to the shed and locking it. "Just get out there and pitch strikes."

By the sixth inning, however, Jesse began to wonder if he would ever pitch another strike again. Just knowing that an eighth grader was behind the plate had made him lose his concentration. His curveball was wild, and his fastball was missing the strike zone. Williamsport had the worst batting in the conference, and still they had managed to drive in two runs. The score stood tied at two apiece.

He had given up two singles and a walk, and now the bases were loaded with only one out. Jesse was so frustrated he felt like throwing his glove down on the mound.

The next Williamsport batter walked out to the plate. He was big, and the only player on the Williamsport team who could really kill the ball. Dennis squatted down and dropped three fingers, signalling the curve. Jesse started from the stretch, set, and pitched, snapping his wrist at the release for spin.

He knew the ball was way low, and his heart skipped a beat. The pitch bounced in the dirt in front of the plate and Dennis dropped to his knees to block it. The ball bounced off Dennis's chest guard, and the runner at third made a move toward home.

Dennis scrambled to the ball, and the runner hustled back to third. Dennis turned to Jesse and gave him an angry stare. It had almost been a wild pitch, and a wild pitch would have let Williamsport score again, and take the lead.

Jesse threw the next two pitches inside for balls, to bring the count to three balls and no strikes.

That's when Dennis ran out to the mound for a conference.

"You're blowing the game, Kissler," Dennis said, glaring at Jesse. "If you throw another ball, you'll walk in a run."

"Lay off him," Josh said, jogging in from third base.

"Why should he?" Justin said, jogging in from second. "You seventh graders are blowing the game for us. If we lose, it's all your fault."

"Yeah, well, you guys are a bunch of . . ." Josh began.

"Everyone shut up!" Jesse said. "Just let me pitch, okay?"

Everyone punched their gloves and went back to their places. It was hard for Jesse to concentrate on pitching when he had so many other things on his mind. He took a deep breath and looked down the alley at Dennis's catcher's mitt.

He wound up and pitched his fastest fastball, right down the middle. The Williamsport batter was all over it, and Jesse watched a well-hit fly ball sail over Nick's head in center field. All three runners advanced, thinking that Nick didn't stand a chance of making the catch.

Nick turned around and sprinted toward the fly

ball. He looked over his shoulder as he ran, faster and faster, pumping his arms. All of the base runners began to slow up on the baseline, to make sure Nick missed the ball.

Nick made an amazing diving catch, snagging the ball as he slid along on his belly. All of the Williamsport runners turned around and scampered back toward their bases as Nick jumped to his feet and whipped a throw to second.

Justin was covering second, and he caught the short-hop throw for the force-out.

The eighth graders went nuts. It had been an incredible double play, and had saved at least three runs.

Jesse and the rest of the seventh graders didn't even clap. They just jogged silently back to the dugout, and sat on the other side of the bench from the eighth graders. It had been an eighth grade double play.

"What's the problem out there?" Coach Lanigan said to the whole team, before the next inning. "We should be creaming Williamsport. Instead, we're fighting for the game. Come on, Panthers. Let's see some spirit."

The Panthers couldn't get anything going at the plate, and the game went into the seventh and final inning all tied up.

Jesse stepped out to the mound ready to pitch. He retired the first two batters on strikeouts. The third batter, however, got hold of a fastball and sent it soaring far over Derrick's head in left field. Jesse could only watch as the Williamsport batter rounded first, second, third, and then headed for home.

The throw from the cutoff man was right on target, but the Williamsport runner slid in under Dennis's tag for the run.

"Safe!" the umpire called, raising his arms.

Jesse slapped his thigh in frustration as he watched the Williamsport bench go crazy. Dennis gave him a steely glance, and whipped the ball back to the mound. Jesse struck out the next batter to get out of the inning—but the damage had been done. Williamsport was ahead by one.

The Panthers needed one run to tie, and two runs to win. Matt was the first at bat, and he grounded out to shortstop. Justin was up next, and he dropped a pop fly into shallow center field for a single.

When Justin crossed first, all the eighth graders cheered. The seventh graders sat in silence, staring at the ground.

Jesse was up next. He tapped the plate with his favorite Bo Jackson bat, and settled into his stance. He knew how important this at bat was.

The pitch looked low, but Jesse swung anyway. His heart dropped when he saw the ball go dribbling along the first-base line, like a bunt. The Williamsport pitcher ran to the ball, bare-handed it, and checked second base. Justin was already sliding into second, so the pitcher threw to first for the easy out. Jesse had advanced the runner, but there was only one more out left in the game.

The whole game, and the whole tournament, rested on Sam's shoulders. The eighth graders were going nuts, cheering Sam on as he stepped up to the plate. Even some of the seventh graders were clapping a little. If Sam got out, nobody would be going to Simpson City.

Sam took the first two pitches for balls, then swung on the third.

Crack!

Everyone on the Panthers' bench shot up and started cheering as the ball sailed deep into left field. Justin crossed home with the tying run, and Sam rounded third. The throw came in from left, but it was too late, and Sam slid across the plate with the winning run.

Sam was mobbed by the eighth graders, who all held up their fingers and chanted, "Number one, number one!" The seventh graders were happy, but they tried not to let it show. It was like they had lost one game, even if they'd won another.

"We rule!" Justin said to Jesse, as they walked toward the locker rooms. "If it weren't for us, you would have lost the whole game."

"Get lost," Jesse said sharply.

Justin looked right at him and laughed.

Just then, B. J. Carruthers walked up to Jesse and tapped him on the shoulder.

"Hey, Jesse," B. J. said, wearing a little smile. "You guys didn't have such a great game, did you?"

"Shut up, Carruthers," Jesse said. "You're just sore because you got cut."

"Did you hear that North Colby won today?" B. J. said. "They're looking pretty good this summer. Better than you guys, in fact."

"Blow off, B. J.," Jesse said, walking into the locker room and slamming the door on B. J.

He had enough things to worry about without having to deal with a sore loser.

7

"Why is Coach making me catch for Sam?" Derrick asked the next day, as he walked toward the storage shed by the baseball diamond. "I don't want to catch for a stupid eighth grader."

Jesse just shrugged. "If you'd been catching for me yesterday, instead of Dennis, I bet I would have pitched great. Instead, I almost blew the game."

"Oh, well," Derrick said, slapping Jesse on the back. "Who cares if the eighth graders won yesterday's game? *We're* going to win the game today."

"If you play great behind the plate," Jesse said, holding his hand out for Derrick to slap, "I promise to slam some homers, and we'll make sure the seventh grade rules the game."

"You've got a deal," Derrick said, smiling and whacking Jesse's hand.

It was another boiling hot day in Cranbrook, and the Alden Panthers were meeting the St. Stephen's team on their home field. Coach had just announced the roster for the day. Sam was starting off on the mound, and Jesse was covering left field. Derrick had been moved in from right field to the catcher's position, and Dennis was covering right.

Jesse wasn't one of the best fielders on the team and he was nervous about being in left field. But Coach couldn't afford to have Jesse sitting on the bench, since he *was* one of the best hitters. Jesse just hoped he didn't get too many plays in the field. That way, he could really shine at the plate.

Coach Lanigan led them to the storage shed. He passed out armloads of bats, gloves, catcher's equipment, bases, and batting helmets to the players waiting at the door. The St. Stephen's team was already on the field, playing pepper and loosening up. Jesse emptied a big green bag of bats in the dugout, while Derrick searched through the catcher's equipment.

"Hey," Derrick exclaimed, looking alarmed and rooting through a big green bag. "My catcher's mitt and my mask are missing. Someone took them."

"You're kidding," Jesse said, as he searched for his Bo Jackson Louisville Slugger bat. Jesse wanted to get in a few minutes of batting practice before the start of the game.

"My shin guards and my chest pad are here," Derrick said angrily, "but nothing else."

"Wait a minute!" Jesse said, feeling his face get hot. "My Bo Jackson bat is gone, too. It's been stolen!"

Josh walked over to his friends and announced that *his* favorite bat was missing, too. The three friends stood in the dugout, fuming. A group of eighth graders walked toward them wearing big smiles.

"That's who did it," Josh exclaimed, pointing. "The eighth graders are trying to make us look bad."

Josh ran up to Sam, with Jesse and Derrick following right behind.

"Give us our stuff back," Josh cried, pushing Sam in the chest. "Now!"

"What stuff?" Sam said, giving Josh a push right back.

"Don't play dumb with us," Jesse answered, looking Nick right in the eyes. "You guys are stealing our equipment to make us look bad."

"What?" Nick said, laughing and shaking his head. "We don't have to prove anything. We already *know* we're better."

Before anyone could say another word, however, Coach Lanigan blew his whistle and called the team over to the bench.

"Listen up, men," Coach started. "We didn't play a very good game yesterday. I don't know what the problem was, but we should have taken Williamsport apart. Now, St. Stephen's is no better than Williamsport. We should be able to beat these guys by five runs, maybe more. I don't want to hear complaints about anything today. Let's just get out there and play ball."

"Coach?" Derrick said, raising his hand. "Someone stole my mitt and my mask."

"Then borrow Dennis's," Coach suggested. "You're on the same team, aren't you?"

Dennis reluctantly gave Derrick his catcher's mitt and mask, and Derrick put them on.

"The glove is way too big," Derrick said to Jesse as they hit the field. "And so is the mask. It's going to totally screw me up. I need my *own* equipment."

Jesse had a good view of the plate from left field,

and he could tell that Derrick was having a bad day. He bobbled easy pitches that he usually would have snagged without even thinking. The Panthers were able to keep St. Stephen's at bay, though, until the third inning, when Sam gave up a single and things got bad.

With a man on first, Sam wound up and pitched. The throw was right across the strike zone, and the St. Stephen's batter took a big cut and missed. But Derrick bobbled the catch, and the ball skipped back toward the backstop. The runner at first saw the passed ball and took off toward second, as Derrick flipped off the mask and scurried back to the ball.

Justin covered second, but the throw was too late and the runner slid in beneath Justin's tag.

Jesse was so mad out in left field that he swore he could feel steam coming out of his ears. The seventh graders were looking stupid on the field. The eighth graders' plan was working perfectly.

Sam pitched a changeup and the St. Stephen's batter stroked a deeper grounder toward Josh at third. Josh bounded toward second base and dived to snag the ball. He jumped to his feet and hurled a throw across the entire infield. It was going to be a close play at first, and Matt was stretched way out, keeping one toe on the bag.

The ball smacked into Matt's glove just as the runner's foot hit the base.

"Safe!" the umpire called.

Jesse kicked at the grass in left field. Now there were runners on first and third, with no outs. Sam pitched another changeup, and as soon as the sound of the ball hitting the bat rang out, Jesse's heart dropped into his shoes.

It was a towering pop fly, hit right toward him. Jesse backed up a little bit, trying to guess where the ball would land, but he went too far back. When he ran forward, it seemed that the ball would land behind him again. So he turned and ran back. The whole time he was running back and forth, the ball was falling fast from the blue sky.

Jesse couldn't run back fast enough and the ball dropped to the ground behind him. He felt his face flush with embarrassment as he scurried to pick up the ball. The runner at third was tagging up, sprinting toward home, and Jesse whipped the ball as hard as he could.

It looked like a perfect throw, one bounce and then right into Derrick's mitt. But Derrick missed the easy catch, and the ball bounced against the backstop. Now there were runners at second and third, and St. Stephen's had taken a 1–0 lead.

St. Stephen's ended up scoring one more run that inning, on another play that Derrick screwed up at the plate. When the inning finally ended, the score was 2–0.

"It's this stupid mitt," Derrick said when Jesse got back to the bench. "It's so big that I can't hold on to the ball."

"Those eighth graders . . ." Jesse said, clenching his teeth.

The eighth graders started a rally in the next inning, driving in a run. With two outs and the bases loaded, Jesse stepped up to the plate. He was too mad to think about batting. Besides, how could anyone expect him to bat well, without his Jackson Louisville Slugger?

Jesse had picked another bat, but it didn't feel quite right in his hands. The handle was a little too thin, and the head was a little too heavy. Jesse knew that he could put the Panthers ahead with a single. He took a few practice swings, then tapped the plate and planted his feet.

It didn't take long. Jesse swung at the first three pitches, and missed all of them by a mile. He angrily tossed the bat to the dirt and grabbed his glove.

"What's wrong with you pipsqueaks today?" Dennis asked Jesse in a snide voice, as they jogged to the outfield. "Looks like *we're* going to have to win the game again."

Jesse made a snide remark in return, but Dennis turned out to be right. The score stayed at St. Stephen's 2 and Alden 1, until the bottom of the seventh inning. Then the eighth grade bats caught fire and the Panthers tied it up with a combination of singles and walks. With men on first and third, Nick whacked a double deep into right field, driving home another run and clinching the game for the Panthers.

The final score was Alden 3, St. Stephen's 2—another eighth grade victory.

"We almost lost again today," Coach said in the locker room after the game. "We should have *creamed* St. Stephen's. I know it's hard for two teams to play together, but you just have to learn to do it. That's why I put an eighth grade catcher with a seventh grade pitcher, and vice versa. We may get through the divisionals playing like we are now, but we sure won't make it in Simpson City. Simpson City will be a different story."

Jesse knew Coach was right, but all he could think about was what jerks the eighth graders were. He couldn't believe they would stoop so low as to steal equipment, and sabotage the seventh grade side.

8

The next afternoon Jesse's mom asked him to take a casserole dish over to the Wilkersons'.

"Mrs. Wilkerson wants to borrow it," she said. "I told her you'd bring it right over."

"But, Mom," Jesse said, "I don't have time. Derrick is coming over right now to work on pitching."

"They live right next door," Mrs. Kissler said. "What's wrong, Jesse? Are you and Nick having a fight?"

Instead of answering, Jesse grabbed the casserole

dish, walked out the door, and stalked across the lawn to the Wilkersons' house. He rang the buzzer, hoping that Mrs. Wilkerson would answer the door, but the footsteps he heard were Nick's.

"What do *you* want?" Nick said, when he opened the door and saw who it was.

"Your mom wanted to borrow this," Jesse said, pushing the dish toward Nick. "I'm surprised she didn't just come over and steal it, because I hear stealing runs in the family."

"Listen, Kissler, we didn't steal your stupid equipment," Nick said, grabbing the dish from his hands. Nick's glasses were getting steamed up. "We won the game because we're *better* than you guys. In fact, if it weren't for the eighth graders, we wouldn't have a chance of making it to Simpson City."

"We'll see about that tomorrow," Jesse said.

"What's that supposed to mean?" Nick demanded, but Jesse had already turned around and run down the steps.

A few minutes later, Derrick showed up at Jesse's with a brand-new catcher's mitt. Jesse was slated to start tomorrow against Lincoln, in the divisional semifinal, and he wanted to make sure his pitching was in top form. The practice would also give Derrick a chance to break in his new mitt.

"I sat on this glove all day, and oiled it, and worked it," Derrick said, crouching down in Jesse's backyard. "But it still feels really stiff. My old mitt was broken in just perfect."

Jesse began throwing his pitches, harder and harder.

"I have to pitch a great game tomorrow," Jesse said, as he prepared to throw his changeup. "We have to show the eighth graders who's in charge."

"I still wish I could catch for you," Derrick said, scooping up a low pitch.

"Me, too," Jesse said. "Pitching to Dennis screws me up."

Jesse hurled his best curveball, and the pitch sank and curved sharply. His arm felt great, and all his pitches were doing just what he wanted them to do. He just hoped he could pitch that well to Dennis in the semifinals.

The game was away, in Lincoln, and the Panthers were supposed to meet the bus in the parking lot of Alden Junior High. When Jesse pulled his bike into the lot the next afternoon, he saw a big group of boys over by the storage shed. As he pedaled closer, he saw that it was a bunch of seventh graders facing off with a bunch of eighth graders, and they looked like they were in the middle of an argument. Jesse squeezed his brakes and stopped by his friends.

"It's all missing, and you stole it," Dennis shouted, pushing Derrick's shoulder.

"Why would we want your lousy catcher's equipment?" Derrick answered, clenching his fists.

"It's the only way you pipsqueaks can make us look bad," Nick said. "But it's not going to work."

"Hey, they stole our bats, too," Justin said, stepping out of the storage shed.

"You guys are really smart," Jesse fumed, stepping off his bike and looking right at Nick. "You steal our equipment, and then you hide your own stuff to make it look like *we* took it."

"Oh, is that what happened?" Nick said, putting his hands on his hips. "I guess you've got it all figured out. Why don't you guys just grow up and give us our equipment back—so *we* can win the game today."

Suddenly everyone got quiet. The boys spotted Coach Lanigan striding toward them from the bus. He looked angry.

"Get on the bus," Coach said, jerking his head toward the parking lot. "Now!"

Everyone climbed onto the bus, the eighth graders in front, and the seventh graders in back. Coach Lanigan stood by the driver with his arms crossed, looking at the team.

"Okay, who's been breaking into the shed and stealing the equipment?" Coach asked. "I want whoever it is to raise his hand."

Everyone looked down, and nobody raised a hand. The bus was dead silent.

"Nobody?" Coach said. "Okay. We'll find out sooner or later. But I want whoever it is to think long and hard about it. He just may be ruining our chances to make it to Simpson City."

When the Panthers took to the field in Lincoln, their team spirit was at an all-time low. Lincoln was a better team than St. Stephen's, and the Panthers couldn't count on good luck to pull them through. The four best hitters on the team were all missing their favorite bats, and Dennis was trying to catch with Derrick's new, stiff mitt—which was too small for Dennis's hand.

Nobody on the entire Panther squad had a good game—except Jesse. For some reason, Jesse was able to forget about everything and throw great pitches. Every curve he threw broke sharply, every changeup hit the mark, and every fastball sped in like a bullet. The only way Lincoln got on base was when the Panther defense erred. Even so, Lincoln wasn't able to get on the board in the first six innings.

Neither was Alden. In the top of the seventh, the

last inning of the game, the Panthers came up to bat with the score still tied at 0–0.

Nick led off the inning. He looked uncomfortable as he took his place at the plate, holding the unfamiliar black bat. Nick took a cut on the first pitch, and the whole Panther bench stood up at the crack of the bat. The ball sailed into deep right field and landed just beyond the reach of the fielder. Nick rounded first and headed toward second.

"No, no," Justin cried. "Turn back!"

Coach was also waving him back to first, but Nick just kept racing for the double. Even though Jesse didn't want to cheer for an eighth grader, he still hoped that Nick would be safe. The Panthers needed to get a rally going.

The throw bounced once and the second baseman snagged it just as Nick dropped into his slide. The Lincoln player swiped his glove across Nick's shins a split second before Nick's foot touched the bag.

"Out!" the umpire called, hoisting his thumb in the air.

Nick jogged back toward the bench all red in the face, and chucked his batting helmet against the fence.

"Nice going, Wilkerson," Josh muttered. "You might have just lost the game for us."

Nick gave Josh a cold stare, and then sat back down with the eighth graders.

Derrick was up next. From the on-deck circle, Jesse watched Derrick strike out for the third time that game. Jesse took a deep breath, knocked the donut weight from the bat, and walked toward the plate.

"Come on, Jesse," Derrick said as they passed each other. "You're the last chance we've got."

With two down and nobody on base, Jesse stepped up to the plate and cocked his bat. It wasn't his Bo Jackson bat, but it would have to do.

Jesse gazed up at the pitcher, trying to guess what he would throw. Jesse figured he'd start out with a fastball, and that's just what happened. The pitch came in low, just where Jesse like it, and he took a big swing—so big, in fact, that he knocked himself off balance and fell to one knee.

"Strike one!" the umpire called.

"Just get a piece of it, Jesse," Coach called from the first base coaching box. "Don't swing too hard."

Jesse didn't want just to get a piece of it. He wanted to knock the ball out of Lincoln. He took another deep breath and settled into his stance. He hoped the pitcher would give him the same pitch. If he did, Jesse was sure he would crush it.

The pitch sped in right around Jesse's knees, and Jesse took the biggest cut of his life. He felt the ball hit the sweet spot and take off over the infielders' heads. Jesse could hear the Panther bench screaming behind him as he dropped his bat and sprinted toward first. Coach Lanigan was spinning his arm around like a windmill, telling Jesse to hurry up and keep running.

Jesse rounded third and headed for home.

"Slide, Jesse, slide," he heard Coach cry out.

The Lincoln catcher was waiting beside the plate, with his mask off and his mitt in the air. Jesse slid headfirst toward the plate and hooked his arm around the catcher's legs. The catcher flipped forward and landed on his stomach, as the throw from right field bounced into the backstop. Jesse slid across the plate, and stood up to meet a whole group of his teammates.

"You saved the game," Josh cried, giving Jesse a bear hug.

Even though Jesse could tell they were happy about the win, the eighth graders didn't come out to congratulate him.

Alden won, 1–0, and the seventh graders could finally chalk up a victory in the feud between the grades.

9

An hour after the game had ended, the bus pulled into the parking lot of Alden Junior High. The eighth graders climbed off first and walked silently to their bikes. Then the seventh graders poured out of the door, still laughing and talking about their victory. Jesse had not only saved the game, he had saved seventh grade pride. More importantly, the Panthers had advanced into the divisional finals.

"Let's do it again tomorrow," Josh said, slapping Jesse on the back. "If we beat North Colby, we're off to Simpson City!"

"North Colby won't be any problem," Derrick said. "Their batting is weak and their best pitcher is injured."

"I'll bet B. J. Carruthers is going to be at the game. He'll be rooting for North Colby all the way," Jesse said.

They decided to celebrate their victory with a large pepperoni pizza at Pete's. Jesse said he knew a shortcut to the Cranbrook Mall. He led his friends into the woods, down a narrow path that cut through tons of bushes and trees.

"Are you sure you know where you're going?" Derrick asked, as Jesse led them deeper and deeper into the woods. "I'm hungry, and I don't feel like taking a nature hike."

"Of course I know where I'm going," Jesse answered, pushing a branch out of the way and letting it snap back against Derrick's chest. "I know these woods like the back of my hand."

The path went up a hillside and then down into a wooded valley, where a creek ran deep and fast. Jesse loved the smell of creeks, and he loved to lift up the big flat rocks and catch the crawdads that hid underneath. The three boys followed the path across the creek, hopping from stone to stone until they reached the other side.

"Wow, look at that!" Derrick said, pointing up the path.

"What?" Jesse asked.

"It's an old fort," Derrick said, starting to run.

A few seconds later, they stopped at a wooden fort that looked like it had been there forever. The windows were broken, and the shingles were crumbling off the roof.

"I wonder who built it," Derrick said.

"I don't know, but it's totally cool," Josh answered.

"Let's look inside," Jesse said, grabbing the door handle and yanking.

When they walked inside the fort, their mouths dropped open. For a second, nobody said a word. They were too amazed to speak.

"It's our equipment!" Jesse said at last.

Sitting in a neat pile in the corner of the fort was everything that was missing from the equipment shed. There was Derrick's mitt and catcher's mask; and Jesse's favorite Bo Jackson Louisville Slugger bat; and Dennis's catcher's equipment, too, and Nick's and Justin's bats. Everything that had been taken from both grades was right there in front of them.

Jesse immediately began to pick up as much equipment as he could carry.

"What are you doing?" Josh asked, putting a hand on Jesse's arm.

"I'm going to take all of this stuff back, so we can use it in the game tomorrow," Jesse answered.

"No, you're not," Josh answered, taking Jesse's bat from his hand and putting it back in the corner. "If *we* bring everything back, the eighth graders will blame it all on us. But we know that they're the ones who are really taking everything."

"He's right," Derrick said. "It sure would look bad if we brought the stuff back."

"What should we do?" Jesse asked.

"Listen up," Josh said. "I've got a plan."

The next morning, Jesse, Josh, and Derrick met at Jesse's house. Josh showed up carrying a paper bag under one arm.

"Is it in there?" Jesse asked, glancing at the paper bag.

Josh just nodded, and gave a little smile.

"Where are you boys going so early?" Mrs. Kissler asked. "The game isn't till this afternoon."

"Oh, we're just going for a walk," Jesse said, trying to look innocent.

"A walk?" Mrs. Kissler said, raising her eyebrows. "Well, whatever you're up to, stay out of trouble."

The three friends rushed out of the door and into the woods at the edge of Jesse's yard. Ten minutes later, after hiking up and down the steep paths, they saw the old fort in the distance and stopped.

"Shhh," Josh said, putting his finger to his lips. "The eighth graders might be around here right now. They can't know that we're here. Let's sneak up and hide in the bushes. We just have to wait until they show up with more equipment."

They moved quickly through the woods, not making a sound, and keeping their eyes out for anything that moved. Jesse could feel his heart racing with excitement. He had never been on a real live stake-out before.

When they got to the big bushes in front of the fort, they pushed aside the branches and climbed quietly inside. There was room for them to sit down and they could see the fort clearly through the leaves.

"Let's see the camera," Jesse whispered excitedly, nudging Josh.

Josh opened up the paper bag and pulled out his father's video camera.

"That looks pretty complicated," Jesse said. "Do you know how to work it?"

"Of course," Josh answered. "When the eighth

graders come, I'll just push this button here and get the whole thing on tape. That way we'll be able to *prove* who's been taking everything."

"Who do you think it is, anyway?" Derrick asked. "Nick?"

"No," Josh said. "I'll bet it's Justin or Sam."

"I guess we'll just wait and see," Jesse said, looking out through the leaves.

An hour passed, and then two. The boys were starting to get restless and bored, all cramped up in their hideout.

"What's that?" Derrick said, all of a sudden. "I hear someone coming."

Josh got the camera ready. Jesse's heart started beating like crazy. He could hear footsteps approaching through the woods, cracking twigs and crunching leaves. He could tell from the sound that it was only one person—but who was it? Sam? Nick?

"I don't believe it!" Josh whispered as he put the camera to his eye. "It's B. J. Carruthers!"

Jesse couldn't believe it, either. B. J. was carrying another armload of Panthers' equipment. At a signal from Josh, the three friends burst out of the bushes screaming. B. J. was so scared he dropped all the equipment and just stood there, staring at them with his eyes wide open.

"So you're the one!" Jesse said, backing B. J. up

against the side of the fort. "We've got it all on tape."

B. J. didn't say a word. He just glared right back at the Cranbrook boys.

"Why did you do this?" Derrick asked, standing right in B. J.'s face.

"Why? Because I think Cranbrook is full of jerks, that's why," B. J. said. "When I moved here, nobody would even say hello to me. So I wanted to see you lose. Especially today, against North Colby."

"I think we should beat him up, and then give the video to the police so they can put him in jail," Josh said, stepping closer to B. J.

B. J. was so scared, he was shaking.

"No," Derrick said, putting his arm out to stop Josh. "I think we should let him go."

"Why?" Josh asked, shaking his head. "He's been taking our stuff."

"I know," Derrick answered. "But I also know what it's like to move into a new place. It's not a lot of fun. I think we should give him a break."

"Oh, come on . . ." Josh began, rolling his eyes.

"I think Derrick's right," Jesse said. He was beginning to feel a little sorry for B. J., too. "Let's just let him go."

B. J. looked incredibly relieved. He turned and ran away through the woods.

"I can't believe you guys just let him go like that,"

73

Josh said, picking up his old bat and giving it a swing. "We should have roughed him up a little."

"We'll rough up North Colby instead," Jesse said.

The three friends picked up all the equipment and hurried off toward the field.

The North Colby game was starting in less than an hour.

10

"I can't wait for the eighth graders to show up," Josh said a few minutes later. Jesse, Derrick, and Josh stood at the storage shed by the diamond, with all the equipment piled up next to them. "I should take a video of their faces."

Just then, Nick, Justin, and Sam rode up on their bikes. When they saw all the equipment, they slammed on their brakes and skidded to a stop.

"I see you guys brought everything back," Justin said, eyeing his bat. "You must have been scared of getting caught."

"Listen, Justin," Josh said, holding up his video camera. "It wasn't us. It was B. J. Carruthers, and we've got it all on videotape to prove it."

"B. J. Carruthers," the eighth graders said, laughing.

"It *was*," Josh said.

"Nice try, Josh," Nick said. "That's the oldest trick in the book. Just blame it on someone else. We're not going to fall for that."

"Come over to my house after the game, and I'll play the tape for you," Josh said. "That'll prove everything."

The eighth graders thought about it for a second.

Finally Nick nodded his head. "We'll come over. But we better see a picture of B. J. stealing the stuff. In the meantime, the eighth graders are going to cream North Colby."

"Oh, yeah?" Josh said, giving Nick a push. "I think the *seventh* graders are going to cream North Colby."

Nick pushed Josh back. Josh swung at Nick, but Jesse stepped in just in time and broke things up. Jesse couldn't believe they were about to play for the divisional title—and that the feud between the grades was still going strong.

The North Colby batter slid his top hand up the bat handle and tapped Sam's pitch down the baseline. It was a surprise drag bunt, and the batter was already on his way to first base when Derrick yanked off his catcher's mask and scrambled out to the ball. There was a base runner at first, and he took off toward second base.

Derrick bare-handed the ball and whipped it to Matt at first base, and the umpire called the runner out. Without missing a beat, Matt pulled the ball from his glove and chucked it to Justin at second base, to try for a backward double play— first base to second. The throw was too high, and Justin jumped for it just as the North Colby runner slid into his legs. Justin missed the catch and did a half-somersault in midair, landing on his shoulder in a cloud of dust.

The North Colby runner saw the loose ball in right field, scrambled to his feet, and rushed toward third. Josh was standing over third base, holding his glove up for the throw from right. The throw bounced once and Josh looked away for a split second—just long enough to lose the ball. It deflected off his legs and rolled into foul territory.

Another overthrow. The runner was on his way home.

Derrick ran out toward the ball, all weighted down with his catcher's gear. He grabbed the ball with one hand just as the runner was passing by him on the baseline. Derrick made an incredible dive toward the runner, holding the ball in his fist. The runner twisted as he ran, trying to avoid the tag, but Derrick laid the ball right on his shoulder.

"Out!" the umpire called.

It was one of the weirdest double plays anyone had ever seen, and it couldn't have come at a better time. Alden was losing, 2–0, and it was already the fifth inning. If Derrick hadn't made that heads-up play, a North Colby runner would have scored on two back-to-back Alden overthrows.

It had been that kind of game. The Panthers were making stupid mistakes in the field—overthrowing first, letting grounders slip between their legs, missing shallow pop flies in the outfield. On the mound, Sam was having the worst day of all. He had already thrown four wild pitches, and had given up eight hits.

Jesse was riding the pine today, so all he could do was cheer for the seventh graders, and hope that the eighth graders didn't screw up their chances to get to Simpson City.

"Come on, Derrick," Jesse said, as Derrick strolled up to the plate in the bottom of the sixth. "Let's get something going. Get a piece of the ball."

Derrick laced a line drive between short and third

for an easy single. Sam was up next, and he drew a base on balls, to put men on first and second with no outs.

Nick popped out to shallow left field, but that didn't dampen Jesse's hopes. There was still only one out, with two runners on base. It was the best chance to score the Panthers had had all game.

Josh stepped up to the plate.

"Whatever you do, keep it out of double play territory," Jesse shouted to Josh, as Josh took his practice swings.

"I'll bet you clowns mess up our best chance all game," Justin said from the bench.

Josh hit an easy grounder right at the third baseman. The North Colby player bent down, fielded the ball, and touched third for the force-out. Then he cocked his arm and chucked a bullet to first base for the double play, and the Panthers' rally was over before it had even begun.

The top of the seventh inning was a disaster. Sam couldn't get the ball over the plate, and he walked the first two batters. The third batter laid down a perfect sacrifice bunt, then beat the throw to first to load the bases.

"Get warmed up, Jesse," Coach Lanigan said, standing up from the bench. "You're going in."

Jesse swallowed hard as he watched Coach jog out to the mound. He was relieving Sam in the worst possible situation—bases loaded and no outs. He could feel a cold sweat breaking out on his forehead.

At least Derrick was catching instead of Dennis. Jesse threw his warmup pitches, and Derrick told him to relax and just do his best. Jesse could tell that the North Colby bench was getting overconfident. They were laughing and joking and taunting the Panthers, certain that they were on their way to Simpson City. Just seeing that got Jesse mad. He couldn't wait to face the first North Colby batter.

Derrick called for a fastball, and Jesse sped one to the inside corner for a strike. The second pitch was a curveball that the batter missed by a mile. The third pitch was another fastball, which the batter deflected into Derrick's glove for the first out.

Jesse was feeling more and more confident. Even the eighth graders were chattering for him to strike another one out.

One, two, three fastballs in a row, and the second batter went down in flames.

The next hitter took a big cut at Jesse's first fastball and hit a towering pop fly. Jesse looked up into the air, shaded his eyes, and called for the play. He didn't even have to move off the mound. The ball fell right into his glove—and Jesse had saved the inning, leaving three North Colby runners stranded.

"Looks like we saved the day," Josh said to Nick, as the team ran off the field for their last at bat.

"Oh, yeah?" Nick said. "Check out the eighth grade bats."

Justin hit a leadoff single, then Dennis hit a double to put men on second and third. When Jesse stepped up to the plate, he wanted to hit a home run so bad he swung too hard, and struck out. The same thing happened to Derrick, and suddenly there were two down with Nick in the batter's box.

The game was coming down to the wire. If Nick made an out, North Colby would take the title to Simpson City.

Nick planted his feet in the dirt and cocked his bat.

Crack!

The Panthers jumped to their feet as they watched Nick's hit sail out beyond the right fielder. Justin scored, and then Dennis rounded third and crossed the plate with the tying run.

Nick was sprinting for the win.

The right fielder reached the ball just as Nick rounded third. He whipped the ball to the cutoff man, who spun around and hurled the ball toward home. Nick made a diving, headfirst slide as the catcher snagged the throw and dropped the tag. For a split second, nobody could tell what had happened because of all the dust.

Then the umpire raised his arms and screamed, "Safe!"

Feud or not, the Panthers were headed to Simpson City.

Coach Lanigan rapped his fist against the clipboard to get the team's attention, but it took a few seconds for the locker room to get quiet.

"Well, we didn't play a great tournament, but we won," Coach said, smiling. "Congratulations. Now I should tell you men something, straight. If we play like this in Simpson City next week, we're not going to last an inning. The competition will be stiffer than anything we've ever seen in the divisionals. We have to learn to pull together and play like *one* team. If we don't, we won't stand a chance."

Coach started to walk away, then turned around.

"One other thing," Coach continued. "You boys need to earn two hundred dollars for the trip to Simp-

son City. If you don't earn it by the time we're sched-
uled to leave, then nobody goes. I know two hundred
dollars is a lot of money. But I think if you pulled
together as a team, you could figure out a way to
earn it."

11

Later that day the eighth graders showed up at Josh's house to watch the video. Jesse hoped that when the video was over—and the feud between the grades was all cleared up—the two sides would sit down together and figure out how to earn the money for the trip to Simpson City.

"This better be good," Nick said. "If we don't see B. J. Carruthers with our equipment, it proves you were stealing it all along."

"But if you *do* see B. J. with all the stuff," Jesse said, "then the feud is officially over. Right?"

Nick nodded.

"Don't worry," Josh said. "I've got it all on tape."

Nick, Justin, Sam, and Dennis all sat on the sofa as Josh put the tape into the VCR. Josh rewound it to the beginning, and then pushed PLAY.

The first thing that came onto the TV was a scene of Josh opening birthday presents with his family.

"It must be just after this," Josh said, looking worried.

But nothing else came on the screen, except Josh holding up a pair of green socks his mother had given him, and smiling a big, stupid smile.

"I thought for sure I pushed the right button," Josh said, sweating. "I swear I did."

"This isn't funny," Nick said, standing up angrily. The other eighth graders stood up, too. "This proves that you guys were stealing everything all along."

"Oh, yeah?" Josh said. "Well, if it wasn't for us, we would have lost the game today."

"Oh, yeah?" Nick said. "*I'm* the guy who hit the home run, in case you forgot."

Nick and his friends headed for the door.

"Wait a second!" Jesse said, trying to calm everyone down. "We have to earn two hundred dollars by

Monday. That's only four days away. We better figure out how we're going to do it."

"We've got our own plans," Nick said. "And we
sure don't need any little kids to help us."

"Oh, yeah?" Josh answered, stepping up in Nick's
face. "Well, we have our own plan, too. And we're
going to make twice as much money as you!"

"We'll see about that!" Nick said, turning and
walking out the door.

The truth was, the seventh graders didn't have a
plan at all. That evening, Jesse, Josh, Derrick, Matt,
and Eddie sat in Pete's trying to figure out how they
were going to earn the money. Jesse was still angry
at Josh for not having turned the video camera on,
and ruining their chance to end the feud. Now they
had to come up with an idea all by themselves.

They thought about having a car wash, but that
didn't sound like fun. They thought about having a
bake sale, but none of them knew how to bake. The
best idea they had was to organize a baseball card
sale.

"A lot of people collect baseball cards," Jesse said,
stuffing half a slice of pizza into his mouth. "And we
have great collections. I bet we could make a thousand dollars."

"When should we hold it?" Eddie asked.

"On Saturday and Sunday," Jesse said. "We'll hold it in the parking lot of the junior high."

"That's a great location," Matt said, getting excited. "And I'm a good sign maker. I'll make a bunch of signs and we can hang them in the mall, and on telephone poles."

"Great!" Jesse said. He was really starting to think that their idea might work. "As long as we can set up in the parking lot, we'll be fine. We need a good location."

"And remember," Josh said, "everyone has to sell some of their best cards. I bet I can get fifteen dollars for my Mickey Mantle."

"And I can get ten dollars for my 1972 Lou Brock," Matt said. "And maybe twenty dollars for my 1966 Frank Robinson."

"All right!" Josh cried, putting his hand out for everyone to whack. "We'll have enough money to make it to Simpson City in no time."

The next afternoon they met at Matt's house, to make signs for the baseball card sale. The more they thought about it, the more they liked their idea. They didn't think anything could mess up their big sale— until Jesse called the junior high to reserve the parking lot.

"We can't have our sale in the junior high parking lot," Jesse said, hanging up the phone. He slumped down in a chair. "The eighth graders have already reserved it."

"What?" everyone said at once. The junior high was the best place to have a sale in all of Cranbrook. It was on the main road, and everyone had to pass by. "Now what do we do?"

"My mom said we could have it in our front yard," Jesse said, shrugging.

Everyone groaned. Jesse's house was on a small, quiet road, and not many people drove by it. It would be hard to get people to come to a baseball card sale there.

"What are the eighth graders planning?" Josh asked.

"They're setting up batting cages in the parking lot," Jesse answered. "They're going to have a bake sale and sell lemonade and iced tea."

"Well, we still have the best sign maker in junior high on our side," Derrick said, slapping Matt on the shoulder. "Let's get to work and make as many signs as we can. We only have one more day before the sale."

The seventh graders spent the next day making signs, and putting them up everywhere they could.

" 'Baseball card sale, in Jesse Kissler's front yard, 26 Concord Ave, Cranbrook, Saturday and Sunday,' " Matt said, reading aloud the sign he had just made. " 'Many valuable cards. Come and help the Alden Panthers get to Simpson City.' "

Early on Saturday morning, all of the seventh graders brought their card collections to Jesse's front yard. Everyone laid their best thirty cards out on folding tables, and put little price tags on them. There were blue and gold banners strung from the trees in the yard, and Jesse's boom-box played a tape of baseball songs. It was a beautiful summer day, and by ten o'clock the seventh grade card sale was open for business.

There was only one problem. No one showed up.

"I can't believe it," Josh said, two hours later. "This is a disaster. We haven't sold one card. We might as well forget about going to Simpson City."

12

Jesse pulled his bike into the parking lot of Alden Junior High. It was later that same afternoon, and Jesse wanted to see how the eighth graders were doing with their batting cages.

The first thing he saw was that the batting cages were empty. The eighth graders were all sitting around, resting their chins in their hands and looking ahead. There were plates of cookies and brownies heaped up on a table near the cages, and it looked like few people had been there all day. Jesse saw

Nick standing all alone by a batting cage and pulled up beside him.

"Hey," Jesse said. "I was just wondering how much money you guys have made."

"Not much," Nick answered, shrugging sadly. "We didn't put up any signs. We figured enough people would pass by. I guess that's why things are so slow. How are you guys doing?"

"Not so hot, either," Jesse answered.

"Well, it looks like we're not going to Simpson City," Nick said, kicking at a stone. "Unless a miracle happens."

"I've been thinking," Jesse said. He climbed down off his bike and sat beside Nick. "Let's end this stupid feud. That's the only way we're going to be able to earn the money."

Nick looked warily at Jesse. "Do you have any great ideas?"

"Maybe we could combine the batting cages and the baseball card sale, and have a big Baseball Carnival," Jesse said.

Nick thought a second. "We could use this location," he mused. "It's still the best in town."

"Matt's a great sign maker, and he can make up a bunch of new signs tonight," Jesse said, getting more excited.

"We could sell all these cookies, too, and we could make more lemonade and iced tea," Nick answered, his eyes lighting up. "I think it's a great idea!"

"The seventh and eighth grade Baseball Carnival," Jesse said. "I like the sound of it."

Nick held out his hand and Jesse gave it a whack.

Jesse grabbed his special Cubs cap and put it on his head.

"C'mon, guys," Jesse said, climbing back onto his bike. "The new Alden Panthers have a lot of work to do!"

That afternoon, all the seventh and eighth graders got together and worked on the Baseball Carnival. Matt and Justin painted new signs while Josh and Sam rode all over town putting them up. Derrick and Dennis spent the evening in Derrick's kitchen, talking about their favorite catchers and baking chocolate chip cookies.

By dinnertime, the whole area was covered with signs for the Cranbrook Baseball Carnival—featuring batting cages, cold drinks, baked goods, and a giant baseball card sale. When all the work was done, the Panthers decided to have a big dinner at Pete's Pizza. They pushed three tables together, and ordered four large pizzas.

"Just think of how great we're going to be in Simpson City," Sam said. "Now that we're one team, the Panthers are going to dominate!"

"If we make enough money to get to Simpson City," Jesse reminded everyone.

"I saw all the signs for the Carnival last night in the mall," Coach Lanigan said the next morning, as he strolled past the tables filled with baseball cards. "I think it's a great idea. I heard a few baseball card collectors over at the mall talking about it, too."

It was only noon, but the parking lot was already filling up with people. There was a big group of men studying the baseball cards and bargaining for better prices. All four batting cages were full, with Jesse, Eddie, Sam, and Duane pitching easy sitters so people could cream the ball. As Jesse pitched, he looked around proudly at the Carnival. Almost all of the cookies had vanished from the bake sale table, and Justin and Josh were pouring the lemonade and iced tea as fast as they could.

A few minutes later, Jesse was walking over to get a drink when he felt a tap on his shoulder. He turned around and saw B. J. Carruthers.

"Hi, Jesse," B. J. said, handing Jesse a small paper bag. "I want you guys to sell this and use the money to help you get to Simpson City."

Jesse opened up the bag and pulled out an old

baseball card, one he instantly knew was very valuable: a 1960 Hank Aaron.

"I don't even know how much it's worth," B. J. went on. "I just hope Alden brings back the state trophy."

"Thanks, B. J.," Jesse said, looking a little confused. "But why did you change your mind about Alden?"

"Well, when you guys caught me taking the stuff, you could have beaten me up and gotten me into a lot of trouble," B. J. answered. "But you didn't. I used to think Cranbrook was filled with jerks, but I guess it isn't."

Jesse watched as B. J. walked away. He was starting to think that maybe B. J. was turning out to be an okay guy.

"How's it going over there?" Jesse called out to Dennis, who was working at the baseball card tables.

"Look!" Dennis said. He opened up an old cigar box and showed Jesse all the money crammed inside.

"Simpson City, here we come!" Jesse said, giving Dennis a big thumbs-up.

13

The Hank Aaron card that B. J. Carruthers gave them turned out to be worth almost a hundred dollars, and a couple of Jesse's cards brought almost twenty dollars apiece. The Panthers earned so much money at the Baseball Carnival that they could afford to buy new uniforms—gold pants with blue socks, and blue-and-gold-striped shirts—for the whole team.

"I can't wait to wear our uniforms in Simpson City Stadium," Nick said to Jesse. They were sitting together on the bus, as it headed north to Simpson City. "Can you believe we're actually going to play in the big stadium tonight, under all the lights? And *you* get to be the starter in the first game."

"I know," Jesse answered, looking out the window at the passing scenery. "I've already got butterflies in my stomach, and we're not even halfway there yet."

"You're going to pitch great tonight," Dennis said, leaning over from the seat behind, and nudging Jesse's arm. "Especially since I'm catching."

Dennis held out his hand and Jesse smiled and slapped it. It was funny how things had changed. Just one week ago, Jesse would have hated the thought of pitching to an eighth grader. But now that the Panthers had become a team, he was psyched to pitch to Dennis.

Later that evening, the team poured into the locker room in Simpson City Stadium. The boys couldn't stop peeking around every corner, and checking out the white rooms with the padded training tables. There were huge showers, and metal lockers with the names of their favorite Simpson City players on them. They were so excited that Coach Lanigan had to blow his whistle three times to get them quiet.

"I know you boys are excited about being in the big leagues," Coach began, as the team gathered around. "When you walk out onto the grass, and see those lights shining down, I know it's going to be hard to concentrate. But we're here to play base-ball—and to win the state invitational trophy. To do that, we've got to concentrate on every pitch, every swing, every hit. Now, Indian Hill is one of the best teams in the state. If we can stop their hit-ters, we'll be okay. It's going to take great pitching, and great fielding. Who's going to win?"

"Panthers!" everyone shouted.

"All right," Coach said, clapping. "Now let's get out there!"

Jesse led the team down the long hallway, up the steps, and out into the bright lights of the stadium. As Jesse ran across the grass toward the Panther bullpen, he thought about all the games that he had watched on TV—games that had been played right on that very same field. He even thought about some of his favorite plays, and imagined them happening right there.

Jesse's arm felt great as he loosened up. It was his stomach that was all tied up in knots. He just hoped he'd be able to handle the pressure of a championship game.

The first Indian Hill batter strutted out to the plate, wearing a red and white uniform. He cocked his bat and gazed up at Jesse from the batter's box. Jesse's heart was pounding as Dennis made the call for the fastball. He took a deep breath, wound up, and hurled.

"Strike one!" the umpire called, as the batter swung and missed.

Maybe these Indian Hill batters aren't as tough as we thought, Jesse thought hopefully, breathing a sigh of relief.

Dennis popped up from the crouch and whipped the ball back to the mound. The whole infield was calling out to Jesse, and the small Cranbrook fan section was cheering as loudly as they could. Dennis called for another fastball, and Jesse pitched. He knew it was a great pitch, speeding in toward the inside corner.

Crack!

The Indian Hill batter had gotten hold of Jesse's best fastball, sending it down the third-base line. Josh scrambled and dived for it, holding out his glove. The ball hit the bag and bounced off at a funny angle. Josh couldn't even touch it. Eddie Peres sprinted over from shortstop and picked up the loose ball. The runner had already made it to first, so

Eddie checked him and threw the ball back to the mound.

The first batter, and I gave up a hit, Jesse said to himself, suddenly feeling worried.

He started from the stretch, set, and checked the runner at first. The runner was taking a big lead, and Jesse got the feeling he was going to steal. Dennis put his catcher's mitt on the far outside corner. If the runner did steal, and the ball came to the outside corner, Dennis stood a better chance of pegging him out at second.

Jesse kicked his leg, and as soon as he made his motion toward the plate, the runner took off for second. When Dennis caught the pitch, he yanked off his catcher's mask and stepped forward to peg the ball. Jesse crouched down on the mound so he wouldn't interfere with the throw, and then turned around to watch the play.

The runner had gotten a good jump on the pitch and was already into his slide by the time Justin caught the peg. But Dennis's throw was perfect and Justin didn't even have to move his glove. He just caught the ball, and the runner slid right into the tag. Alden had made the perfect pickoff play.

The Panthers threw the ball around the horn, and Jesse felt his confidence come back. It helped knowing that he could count on his team for great fielding. All Jesse had to do was carry his own weight against the Indian Hill batting powerhouse.

Jesse struck out the next batter on a curveball. The third batter smacked a sharp grounder to Sam at second. Sam ran toward first and snagged the ball on the short hop. He turned and threw the ball to Matt for the third out, and the Panthers were out of the first inning without any damage.

Indian Hill's pitching was better than the Panthers had expected. The Alden batters were having a hard time sending runners across the plate. After five innings, the Panthers had left a total of seven runners stranded on base, and Jesse could tell that Coach was getting nervous. It seemed like every inning ended with a classic choke. Jesse stepped up to bat in the top of the sixth—with the score Indian Hill 1, Alden 0. He decided it was time to end the choking.

They were two down, and Matt was at first base on a walk. Jesse adjusted his helmet and looked up at Coach Lanigan in the first base coaching box. Coach crossed his arms, licked his fingers, pulled his ear, and then tipped his hat, giving the sign. Jesse nodded once and stepped up to the plate. Coach had just signalled to him that Matt was going to steal second base, and that Jesse should hit out on the pitch.

The pitcher set, checked Matt at first, then made his motion toward the plate. The pitch came speeding in low around the knees—just where Jesse liked it. Jesse took a cut and felt the meat of the bat smack the ball.

He dropped his bat and ran toward first, watching the ball float out into deep right field. The Indian Hill outfielder turned, sprinted back toward the ball, and made a diving leap. The ball disappeared and Jesse's heart sank. Then the player did a somersault on the ground, and Jesse saw the ball roll out onto the grass.

"Go, Matt!" Jesse cried, as he headed toward second.

Matt had gotten a great jump on the pitch, and was already rounding third and heading for home by the time the outfielder got control of the ball. He sprinted down the third-base line, pumping his arm as hard as he could, and keeping his eyes fixed on the plate. The throw came in high, and the catcher jumped to snag it. Matt made a hook slide and the catcher brought the tag down a split second late.

"Safe!" the umpire shouted.

Jesse rounded second, and started toward third.

"Stop, Jesse," Coach yelled behind him. "Stay at second!"

Jesse heard Coach, but he didn't stop. Jesse knew he wasn't the fastest player on the team—but he was so excited that he couldn't help but go for the big triple.

The Indian Hill catcher yanked the ball back and whipped it to third base. Jesse saw the throw come in even before he started his slide, and knew that he had made a mistake. The best that he could hope for now was to knock the third baseman down and to jar the ball from his glove.

Jesse dropped and slid, and felt the tag swipe across his thigh.

"Out!" the umpire called.

Why didn't I just stay at second? Jesse thought, slapping his thigh in frustration as he ran back to the dugout. *Maybe the next batter would have batted me in.*

With the out, the Panthers took to the field again. At least Jesse had batted in the first Alden run of the game. The score was tied at 1–1. He just hoped that his baserunning didn't come back to haunt the team later.

It was the top of the last inning, and Jesse's arm was starting to get tired. He could tell he was beginning to lose his control. After he walked the first two batters, Coach Lanigan jogged out to the mound.

"How's your arm?" Coach said. "Do you want Sam to relieve you?"

Jesse shook his head. He had taken the Panthers this far in the game, and he wanted to finish it himself. Coach slapped him on the shoulder and told him to keep the ball low.

Jesse pitched the next batter a low fastball. If he threw the ball low, the batter was more likely to hit a ground ball into the infield, which the Panthers could convert into a double play. The batter swung, and shot a bullet grounder right back at Jesse on the mound.

It was all pure reaction. Jesse twisted around, dropped to one knee, and snagged the grounder. If he had missed it, the ball would have rolled into center field, and the man on second might have scored. Instead, Jesse jumped to his feet, and chucked the ball to Eddie, who was running toward second from shortstop. The ball met Eddie at the base, and Eddie caught it, stepped on the bag, and hurled the ball to Matt at first—in the same motion. Matt was stretched out as far as he could with his toe barely on the bag. He snagged the ball on the short hop for the double play.

Jesse had only one more out to make. Then the Panthers would get their chance to break the tie.

He started from the stretch, set, and checked the runner at third. Josh was covering the base, holding his glove up. Jesse wanted to make the runner work a little, so he spun around and threw the ball to Josh. Instead of diving back to the base, the runner made a crazy dash for the plate.

Josh ran after him down the baseline, and Dennis yanked off his mask to get ready for the throw. Jesse ran back behind the plate, to back up the play in case something went wrong.

Josh whipped the ball to Dennis, but the throw was too high. Dennis jumped, missed the ball, and the Indian Hill runner closed in on home. Jesse was backing up the plate. He dove and snatched the over-throw, then scrambled to his feet and leaped toward the plate just as the runner slid. They crashed into each other, like two linemen on the football field.

"Out!" the umpire called.

The Panthers cheered and ran back to their dug-out. All they needed for the win was a single run.

Nick stepped up to bat, and creamed the first pitch down the right-field line. The whole Panther bench was on their feet in a second. Nick had good speed, and everyone could tell that he was gunning for an inside-the-park homer.

When Nick rounded third, the Panther team started jumping out of the dugout and running toward the plate, leaping and cheering. The throw from right field was too high, and the ball went over the catcher's head. Nick didn't even slide. He just jumped onto the plate with both feet, lifted his arms, and was mobbed by the Panther squad.

Jesse was the first one to maul Nick, and the two friends let out a huge banshee cry. They were on their way to the finals.

14

The sound of the small crowd echoed throughout the stadium. Out on the mound, the Panthers lost the coin flip, and Crawford won the home team advantage. They would get to bat last. The pressure was on the Panthers to put a lot of runs on the board before the bottom of the seventh inning. If they didn't, Crawford might steal the game—and the championship.

Coach Lanigan stood in the dugout, giving his team a last minute pep talk.

"We've come a long way to get here, men," Coach

started, pacing back and forth. "Last night we played one of the best games we've ever played. I was proud of every one of you. But tonight is the most important game of all. If we win tonight, we take home the biggest trophy Alden Junior High has ever seen. We have to get out there and play our game. We have to keep our heads on straight, and not make stupid mistakes. No overthrows, no bobbled pop-ups, no grounders that go through the legs. Crawford has the best batting in the state. Our defense is going to have to be sharp. And our batting is going to have to be better than ever. Who's going to win?"

"Panthers!" the whole bench shouted in reply.

Jesse was on the bench tonight. He had done his work the night before, and now it was Sam's turn to pitch. He wished he could be out there, pitching and batting. Still, he knew that his arm was tired, and that Sam was Alden's best bet. Jesse cheered as Josh led off with a sharp single to left-center field. But Josh was left on base at the end of the inning.

Jesse could tell that Sam was having trouble from the start. Derrick was behind the plate, and every few pitches he'd run out to the mound and have a little conference with Sam. Sam walked the first two batters, and then gave up a deep single to drive in Crawford's first run of the game.

Now there were men at first and third, with one

out. Jesse held his breath as Sam went into his windup and pitched. One thing he knew for sure was that the Panther fielding was the best in the state. If anything could save the inning, it was Alden's defense.

Crack!

Nick dashed in from center field and grabbed the ball on the second hop. The runner at third headed for home, but he didn't know about Nick's arm. Without missing a beat, Nick snatched the ball from his glove and chucked it as hard as he could. Derrick was waiting at the plate, caught the throw, and tagged the runner out for a beautiful play.

Nick's heads-up ball playing had just kept Crawford from scoring their second run. But there was nothing the fielders could do when Sam walked the next player, to load the bases.

"Come on, Sam," Jesse shouted from the dugout. "Show Crawford some fire. Smoke it in there!"

Sam's first two pitches were balls. When he pitched another ball, Derrick jogged out to the mound to cool him down. But whatever Derrick said, it didn't work. The next pitch was ball four, and the Crawford runner at third trotted across the plate to score the second Crawford run.

Sam kicked at the rubber in frustration. The next

Crawford batter stepped up to the plate with two down and the bases still loaded. The first pitch was a called strike, low and inside, and the Panther cheering section started making some noise. The next pitch was a fastball down the middle, and the batter swung and missed for strike two.

The next three pitches were balls, to bring the count to three balls and two strikes. One more ball and another Crawford runner would stroll across the plate.

Sam set, checked the runners, and pitched. It was a perfect changeup and the batter swung way too early for strike three. It took a lot of guts to throw a changeup on a full count with the bases loaded. Sam was a gutsy pitcher. The inning was over, and Alden was down by two runs.

Sam gave up a few hits in the next five innings, but Crawford wasn't able to drive them home. Jesse thought that Sam had really settled down since the first inning. He was pitching a solid game.

The Alden defense had pulled through in the clutch, but the Panther offense was getting smoked by Crawford's pitching. When the Panthers came up to bat in the top of the sixth, the score was still Crawford 2, Alden 0.

Nick led off with a stand-up double to right, and

the Panther bench started cheering for a rally. Then Matt struck out, and so did Eddie. Suddenly the hopes for a rally began to fade. Derrick was batting cleanup for Alden, and he was up next.

"Come on, Derrick," Jesse cried, cupping his hands and standing up in the dugout. "Get a piece of the ball."

Nick was taking a big lead from second, and on the pitch, he broke for third. The Crawford catcher made a good throw, but Nick was just too fast. He slid safely into third for a big stolen base.

Jesse looked over to Coach Lanigan, and watched his hand signals. He couldn't believe what he saw. Derrick was supposed to try a squeeze bunt.

When the pitcher wound up, Derrick squared off and choked up on his bat for the bunt. Nick started down the baseline, waiting to see what happened. If Derrick missed the pitch, Nick would hustle back to third. But if Derrick laid down the bunt, Nick would sprint for home.

The whole infield saw Derrick squaring off, and rushed toward the plate.

Derrick tapped the ball right down the third-base line, and Nick picked up his speed. The Crawford third baseman kept running toward the bunt and he bare-handed the ball, chucking it home as he ran.

Nick was already into his headfirst slide, and was across the plate before the catcher could drop the tag.

It had been a textbook squeeze bunt, and Derrick was safe at first. The Panthers had finally gotten on the board.

That was all they'd get that inning. Sy was up next and he grounded out to second base for the third out. The Panthers went into the bottom of the sixth with the score Crawford 2, Alden 1.

Jesse could tell that Sam was worn out. He walked the first batter, then gave up a single to put runners on first and third. He walked the next runner, and the bases were loaded.

These next pitches were incredibly important. The Panthers only had one more at bat left. Any runs that the Panthers gave up now would have to be made up in one inning—and Crawford wasn't in the habit of giving runs away.

Sam pitched a low fastball, and the batter swung on. The ball was hit sharply toward Justin at second base. Justin jumped for it, but the hit was just out of his reach. The Crawford runner ran easily from third base to the plate, and all the other runners advanced as well. Sam hit his glove against his thigh in frustration, as the scoreboard changed to read

Crawford 3, Alden 1. The state championship was slipping through Alden's fingers.

That was when Coach Lanigan strolled out to the mound.

Jesse watched the conference on the mound, and wondered what they were saying. He knew that he might be called on to relieve Sam. It would be exciting to get in there and pitch in the state championship game with the bases loaded and all of it riding on every single pitch. He knew that heroes were made at moments like this. On the other hand, if he screwed up, it could cost them the championsip.

Jesse's heart was pounding like crazy as he watched Sam start to walk off the field.

Coach pointed to Jesse in the dugout, and waved for him to take the mound. Jesse stood up and grabbed his glove.

"All right, Jesse," the Panthers said, encouraging him.

"Just take it easy and pitch us out of the inning," Sam said. "We'll take care of the rest."

Jesse slapped Sam's hand.

"They're pretty tough at the plate," Sam added. "Good luck."

Jesse nodded, swallowed hard, and walked out to the mound.

15

Jesse had never been so nervous in his whole life. When he got to the mound, Coach Lanigan and Derrick were waiting for him. Jesse held out his glove and Coach Lanigan dropped a new game ball into it.

"Okay, big guy," Coach said, looking Jesse in the eye. "We're down to the wire. Keep your cool and get us out of this inning. Remember to keep the pitches low. We want them to hit into a double play."

"Or a triple play," Derrick added, trying to calm Jesse down.

"Just make sure you two protect the plate," Coach added. "Relax and throw your best pitches. Let the Panther defense take care of the rest."

Coach walked off the field, but Derrick stayed behind for a moment longer.

"Just pretend we're in your backyard," Derrick said.

Jesse smiled and nodded. Derrick was a good catcher—not just because he knew how to handle pitches, but because he knew how to handle pitchers. Derrick knew exactly how to calm Jesse down.

The Crawford batter walked to the plate, and Jesse started from the stretch. He knew he had to keep the ball low, to force the batter to hit a grounder.

He kicked and pitched a changeup, wide for ball one. The batter fouled off the next two fastballs to bring the count to one and two. Jesse liked getting out ahead of the batter in the count. He knew that the batter would have to swing at the ball if it was anywhere near the strike zone, and sometimes that batter would take a cut at a bad pitch. Unfortunately, Jesse didn't get the next two fastballs into the strike zone, and suddenly he was pitching with a full count.

If he threw a ball, another run would score, and the trophy would slip that much further out of Alden's reach.

Jesse looked down at Derrick's signal—one finger, and that meant a fastball. Jesse nodded, set, and checked the runners at first and third. His heart was beating wildly. He kept reminding himself to keep the ball low—but not *too* low.

He kicked and hurled the ball right toward Derrick's mitt. The batter took a cut, but he topped the ball, sending a grounder to Josh at third. Josh snagged it on the short hop, and chucked the ball right back to Derrick, for the force-out at the plate.

Derrick caught the throw, stepped on the plate, and whipped the ball down the line to first base. The throw was perfect and Matt made the catch for the double play.

Jesse leaped into the air and swung his fist. The double play couldn't have come at a better time. Jesse felt his confidence building and building.

He struck out the next batter and saved the inning.

The celebration didn't last long, though, because the Panthers knew what a huge task they had before them. They were down 3–1 in the top of the seventh and last inning. They needed at least three runs for the win, and they needed them *now*.

"Take your best cut, Jesse," Coach said, as Jesse adjusted his batting helmet. "If there ever was a time to swing out, this is it. Go for everything."

Jesse nodded and walked out to the plate. The big

stadium lights were glaring down, and the night was steamy. Jesse was hot, and he could feel the sweat running down his cheeks as he cocked his bat. He gazed up the alley at the Crawford pitcher, and the pitch came in low—just where Jesse liked it.

The ball curved at the last second, and Jesse swung and missed for strike one.

You can't strike out now, Jesse thought, stepping back into the batter's box. *Just get on base any way you can.*

The next pitch looked a little high, but Jesse went for it anyway. He didn't get much on the ball. It looped up over the shortstop's head and dropped into left field for a single.

"Good stroke, Jesse," Coach said as the Alden fans started cheering louder and louder. "Now just take it easy on the bases. Run smart and listen to what I say."

Josh was up next. Jesse looked into the outfield and saw the fielders moving up and playing Josh shallow. Even though Josh wasn't a big kid, he had a surprising amount of power. Jesse just hoped Josh would show his power now, when it really mattered.

Josh swung on the first pitch and cracked a high fly ball into right field, way over the right fielder's head. Jesse took off running as fast as he could. Josh

had really burned the Crawford outfield. As Jesse
crossed second he looked behind him and saw that
the ball was still loose in left.

"Keep running!" Coach cried out.

Jesse tried to make his legs move faster.

"Slide, Jesse!"

Jesse dove and slid headfirst into third—just beating the tag. Josh had made it to second with a stand-
up double.

Everyone could feel it—the Panthers were on a
roll.

The Crawford coach decided to give the next batter—Justin—an intentional walk. If the bases were
loaded, then Crawford could get a force-out at any
base—including home plate. The catcher stood up,
held his mitt out beside him, and the pitcher lobbed
the ball wide. After four pitches, Justin tossed his
bat aside and jogged to first, to fill up the bases.

Even though the stadium was almost empty, the
cheering was the loudest Jesse had ever heard—at
least when *he* was on the field.

Kyle Bushmiller stepped up to the plate with the
bases loaded and no outs. He had a look of intense
concentration on his face as he swung at the first
pitch, missing for strike one. He swung at the next
pitch, too, and missed again. The third pitch was

way low, but Kyle went fishing for it, and whiffed for the first Panther out.

Dennis was next, and he hit an easy pop fly to shallow center field for the second out.

The Crawford team was getting excited. All they needed was one more out, and they would win the championship—and Alden would go home with a runner-up trophy. Jesse stood on third base and put his hands on his hips. The bases were loaded, and Jesse couldn't stand the thought of losing when they had come so close to pulling off an amazing comeback.

"Let's see it, Nick!" Jesse called out, clapping his hands. "Knock it out of here!"

Nick took the first two pitches for balls. Since there were two down, the runners were going on anything. On the third pitch, Nick took a big cut and knocked the ball deep into left field. Jesse took off toward home and crossed the plate. He turned around to watch the play in the outfield, and started spinning his arm to signal Matt to come home with the tying run.

The ball was still rolling toward the wall when the Crawford fielder finally picked it up and chucked it to the cutoff man. Matt crossed home and Jesse kept circling his arm faster and faster, and screaming to Justin to come in. Justin was halfway down the baseline when the cutoff man whipped the ball to the plate.

It was going to be a close one.

"Slide!" Jesse shouted.

Justin dropped and the throw was high. The catcher had to jump to reach it, and by the time he landed and laid the tag, Justin had already touched the plate. The Panthers had pulled ahead by one!

Jesse and Matt and Justin all hugged at the plate and ran back to the dugout. Jesse looked over to Nick and gave a big thumbs-up. Nick stood on third, beaming.

Eddie was up next, and he struck out to end the inning.

The Panthers took the field in the bottom of the seventh, ahead by the score of 4–3. If they could shut out Crawford this inning, they'd take home the state trophy.

"Just take it easy out there," Coach said to Jesse on the mound. "Pitch your best."

Jesse struck out the first batter with three fastballs. The next batter didn't give up so easily.

The Crawford batter got hold of a curveball and chopped a hard line drive toward Matt at first. Matt dove for the ball, but it hit the butt of his mitt and bounced out. He tumbled into the dirt, then scrambled to his feet, grabbed the ball, and sprinted off toward first, beating the runner to the bag by half a step.

Jesse's head was beginning to ring. He was so excited that he hoped he could just get the ball over the plate. One more out and the Panthers were the state champions.

Jesse pitched a changeup but the batter wasn't fooled. He swung on and hit a towering pop fly, way up into the lights. It looked like it would land right on the mound. Jesse shaded his eyes and called, "MINE!!"

The ball was a little dot way up in the lights of the stadium. Jesse took a few steps off the mound and waited, looking up. The ball seemed to take forever to fall, and a thousand thoughts crowded into Jesse's head. He pictured the headlines of the *Cranbrook News* saying *Panthers Win State Title in Simpson City*. He imagined how the big trophy would look in the trophy case at Alden Junior High, and how proud the whole school would be.

Then the ball flew down, right into Jesse's glove! A second later, he was mobbed on the mound by the entire Panther squad.

Pro Set Cards
and the
Alden All Stars
present
THE ALL STAR SWEEPSTAKES

- **Grand Prize: a trip for two to the 1992 Pro Bowl in Hawaii**

- **First Prize: a *complete* set of Pro Set's 1991 Series I and II—the *official* card of the NFL. Complete sets are not available in stores.**

- **Two Second Prizes: all of the books in the Alden All Stars series—nine books in all!**

OFFICIAL RULES—NO PURCHASE NECESSARY

ALL STAR SWEEPSTAKES OFFICIAL ENTRY FORM

Name _____ Age _____

Address _____

City/State/ZIP _____
(please print)